Face of Guilt

by

Kathy Ecenbarger

ZONDERVAN PUBLISHING HOUSE
Grand Rapids, Michigan

Dedicated to
Dr. Harold L. Fickett, Jr.
For the Sermon He Wasn't Afraid
to Preach

CHAPTER ONE

THE LITTLE BIRD popped through the open door in the face of the clock and proudly announced the time with eight loud cuckoos. Mrs. Templeton looked up from her cup of tea. She never tired of watching and listening to her little friend. Little friend? It was funny, but in a way that bit of wood and paint did seem like a friend.

She always enjoyed twelve o'clock because then she could watch the cuckoo the longest. Those few seconds brought back memories of her son, Richard. The clock was the last thing he had sent her from Germany — just before he was killed.

The little bird finished his announcement and slipped back into the clock. Mrs. Templeton drained the last drops of tea from her cup. Eight o'clock. Time to go in and sit by the front window. Across the street Mr. Rosenthal would be ready to open his grocery store. She had watched him accomplish this task faithfully for the last ten years. He never missed a day. Rain, shine or holiday made no difference. Come eight o'clock, he opened his door.

Mrs. Templeton set the empty cup down and pushed herself painfully to her feet. With slow, shuffling steps, she moved into the living room and eased herself into the chair by the window.

Movement was going to be difficult today. Some days were like that. Other days she had very little trouble with her arthritis. Really, she couldn't complain. At least she was able to take care of herself. That was saying a lot for a woman of seventy-two.

Twisting slightly in the chair to get a better view, she saw that Mr. Rosenthal had already opened his front door and was fastening it with a piece of wire. Years ago some prankster had stolen his wooden doorstop. He had never replaced it. Mrs. Templeton still laughed when she thought about it. He had been so mad. He just didn't appreciate a joke if money was involved.

When he finished with the door, Mr. Rosenthal glanced up at the sky briefly, then disappeared inside the store. His day had begun. Unless she crossed the street to do some shopping, Mrs. Templeton wouldn't see him again until he locked up at six o'clock.

Today would be a busy day at the store. It was the first of the month. The old neighborhood was home to a great many pensioners and they all received their government checks on the first. Mr. Rosenthal kept an extra supply of money on hand to cash those checks. He didn't even charge to do it. Of course, Mrs. Templeton thought, he had his motives. When they came to cash their checks, they always bought a few groceries.

Who would be the first customer of the day? This was a game she played each morning, although today it really wasn't fair to play. She knew who the first customer would be. On the first of the month it was always Marvin Clark. Poor Marvin. The poor boy.

Boy . . . how silly to think of him as a boy. He was close to fifty. To her, he would always be a boy. Every time she saw Marvin she remembered how he used to tear up and down the sidewalk on his roller skates, scaring the daylights out of folks on foot. Then there were the times he and Richard used to chase the girls with mice and worms. Where had time gone? All those years.

The boys had gone to war together. How proud they had been in their uniforms — and how handsome. They left together, but Richard hadn't returned. He had died in a field in Germany. Marvin . . . he came back; but he wasn't the same Marvin. They called it shock. He hardly spoke to anyone. They said he even yelled and screamed in his sleep. And drink! Almost his whole pension check went for liquor. What a pity, Mrs. Templeton thought. If there was only something that could be done for him.

As she sat watching, a car drove up and stopped in front of the store. This was strange. The store was off the main street. Not many people drove to it. Most of the customers were neighborhood people who walked.

She saw two young boys get out of the car and go into the store. They looked like nice young boys. She didn't see many young people any more, and she couldn't recall seeing these boys before. What were they doing here?

An idea came to her and her thoughts drifted from the boys to the car. Here was a chance to practice the letter game. Little Susan from next door was sure to come over to play it with her this evening.

In the evening they would sit together in front of the window and watch for cars to pass on their way home from work. Each car license plate had three letters. She and Susan would try to make up sentences with words beginning with each letter. It was a silly game, but Susan loved to play it. It did help to pass the time.

MBC. She thought for a moment. *MBC. Martha begs candy. No, that would never do.* Susan could easily beat that. *Martha bopped Cindy. There had to be a better sentence. Mother bakes cookies. Well . . .? Yes, that was better. Mother bakes cookies. Susan would have to work to beat that.*

A loud commotion across the street interrupted her thoughts. One of the boys came running out of the store. He grabbed at the car door and yanked it open. Just as the door opened, the driver started the car. Mrs. Templeton caught her breath. If the driver started off now the boy getting in was sure to fall beneath the wheels.

Things began to happen too fast for Mrs. Templeton to follow. The other boy came running from the store. Mr. Rosenthal appeared and was waving something in his hand.

The boys must have forgotten a package. One of the boys turned back, but he didn't take the package. Instead he grabbed Mr. Rosenthal by the arm.

What was this? The two seemed to be fighting. Why would they fight? The second boy joined the struggle. All three of them fell to the sidewalk, and then there was a loud noise.

As suddenly as the fight began, it stopped. For a moment the three bodies remained still. Then arms and legs began to untangle. From her window, Mrs. Templeton watched. She forgot momentarily that what she was seeing was actually happening and was not another television program.

One boy scrambled to his feet. He helped the other one up. They looked down at Mr. Rosenthal, and stood there a long time, or so it seemed. She wished one of them would offer to help Mr. Rosenthal up. Maybe then he would forgive them.

The two boys jumped into the car. Before they had time to pull the door shut, the car was speeding down the road. Mrs. Templeton watched until it screeched around the corner.

When the car went out of sight, she turned her attention back to Mr. Rosenthal. He was still lying on the sidewalk. He hadn't moved. Why didn't he get up? Didn't he know it was safe now? He was lying so still.

She stirred uneasily in her chair. What was wrong? What should she do? She felt terribly confused. What had happened? They were such nice-looking boys. Surely they wouldn't have hurt Mr. Rosenthal. Maybe she should go see. It was such a long way across the street. Probably nothing serious had happened. Still . . . he hadn't moved the least little bit. And the poor man had absolutely no one to take care of him. She had better go see.

Slowly she got to her feet. The pain was still there. Down the steps and across the street would be a difficult trip. Her determination wavered, but only for a moment.

At the hall closet, she paused. Should she take her

purse? There were a few things she needed from the store. No, that wouldn't do, she thought, shaking her head. If Mr. Rosenthal was really hurt he needed help right away.

Stepping outside, she purposely left the front door open just a crack so she could get back in easily. From the outside the door was hard to open. One at a time, she went down the ten steps to street level. Just as she reached the sidewalk, she saw Mr. Jenson come out of his rooming house next to the store. She was about to call to him to help her with Mr. Rosenthal, when he noticed the crumpled figure on the sidewalk.

Running over to the body, Mr. Jenson bent down and started to turn Mr. Rosenthal over. Then he stopped. He straightened up and ran into the store.

Mrs. Templeton reached the other side of the street and started toward Mr. Rosenthal. Now what should she do? Mr. Jenson was inside the store and was probably calling for help. Was there anything she could do? She looked down at Mr. Rosenthal as she drew closer. A gasp escaped her lips as she stared in disbelief. Mr. Rosenthal was lying in a pool of blood. An inner instinct, which comes with age, told her that he was beyond help. The grocer was dead.

She stood still. The events she had witnessed began to fall into place. *The car . . . the three boys . . . oh, but surely those boys couldn't have done this . . . they looked like such nice boys . . . yet . . . who else could have done it?* She had seen the boys tussling with Mr. Rosenthal. Now the poor man was lying on the sidewalk — dead.

Mr. Jenson came out of the store. He said something, although she didn't understand what it was. So many thoughts were tumbling through her mind. One thought seemed to return again and again. How could such nice-looking boys have done such a terrible deed? No, she scolded herself, she mustn't condemn them. Perhaps what she had seen wasn't exactly right. Perhaps Mr. Rosenthal had fallen. There were times when she knew she got things confused. Yes, that sounded right. He had fallen and bumped his head. Those nice boys probably didn't even know he was hurt. It was all an accident. An accident? No, she knew it wasn't an accident.

A police siren sounded in the distance. Its wail grew louder and louder. Suddenly it stopped. A policeman appeared at her side. He smiled at her as he helped her inside the store to a chair. It was such a relief to sit down. With all the confusion, she hadn't realized how tired her legs had become.

The policeman started asking her questions. It was hard to follow what he was saying. Her mind was so foggy. He wanted to know what she had seen.

With effort, Mrs. Templeton managed to clear her mind. She had seen the car and the three boys. They were nice, clean-cut boys. No, she couldn't recall what they looked like. They had gone into the store and come out. There had been a struggle on the sidewalk. That was all that had happened.

Did she know any of the boys?

No, she had never seen any of them before.

Had she seen anything that might be of help in finding the murderers?

"Murderers!" Mrs. Templeton looked up at the policeman in shock. "Surely those boys couldn't have murdered Mr. Rosenthal. It must have been an accident." The policeman shook his head. It hadn't been an accident.

Was there anything else she might remember? Perhaps some seemingly unimportant item?

The policeman was being so nice, she wished she could think of something else. Slowly she shook her head. She had told him everything.

He thanked her and started away. A thought flashed into her mind. *Mother bakes cookies . . . MBC . . . could that be of help? Half a license plate? It might help. Poor Mr. Rosenthal. How terrible to be murdered.* She hated to hurt the young boys. She didn't even know them. But Mr. Rosenthal. . . .

14

"Mother bakes cookies." She called out to the police-man. There was something else she remembered.

The policeman turned back toward her. He had a quizzical look on his face. Then Mrs. Templeton realized that she hadn't completed her sentence. "MBC. Mother bakes cookies. Those were the letters on the license plate of the car." She started to explain the little game to the policeman but he dashed from the store in a hurry. She was left alone again. Why must everyone be in such a hurry?

CHAPTER TWO

GARY WILSON EASED his car into the heavy flow of evening traffic. He disliked driving in slow, stop and go traffic, but he had to be careful. He didn't want to have any accidental meeting with the law.

He threw a lock of unruly hair off his forehead with a cocky twist of his head. It had gone pretty well this morning. The only hitch was Mark having to hit the old man. Too bad it had been Mark. He was such a moralist. Gary hoped the old man wasn't hurt. That hadn't been a part of their plan. The old guy had scared them — running out and waving that gun. They hadn't meant to hurt anyone.

A slow breath escaped his lips. It was over. It had been interesting — like a lab experiment. Now it was over. So what if it happened? It didn't make any difference. The feeling of boredom was returning. How he hated that feeling. Nothing mattered. Nothing was worth caring about. Nothing was worth living for. Nothing . . . nothing.

Boredom! That's what had caused the whole thing. Too bad about the old guy. Too bad Mark had been the one. Mark! Gary had forgotten all about his friend. Mark hadn't said a word since they'd dropped John off. He glanced over at him.

"Relax, Mark, it's over," Gary kidded. "If a cop came along right now he'd arrest you on general principles because you look so guilty."

"Wha . . . oh." Mark sat up straighter, then sagged back down. "I wasn't even thinking about it." He was quiet for a moment as he sought words. "I was thinking . . . well it's over.' We planned it; we did it; and it's over. Just like that. Just like nothing. It seems. . . . well it seems like it never happened."

That's it, Gary thought. They were the same thoughts he'd had. He wasn't the only one to feel this nothingness.

Mark went on. "While we were planning it, I really got excited. It doesn't seem like it should end. What have we proved? What are we going to do now?"

What did come next? Gary, too, wondered. How could a guy get so tired and bored with life before he was even eighteen? Life was only bombs, wars, sex, crime and nothingness. It didn't take long for a guy to find out that there really wasn't much to this thing called life.

"Oh, well," Gary sighed, "it'll be fun watching the cops run around in circles trying to solve this thing."

"Guess so," came Mark's weary reply. "Maybe I'm disappointed because it's over. At least it was something to do."

This time Gary didn't reply. What could he say? Their generation seemed destined to be bored to death. Nothing was asked of them — nothing demanded — no challenges. All they were expected to do was take everything given them and appreciate it.

"Where did you leave your car?" Gary asked, breaking the silence.

"Behind Week's Department Store."

"I'll let you off at the corner."

Mark nodded.

"There's a newsstand," Gary pointed. "I'll slow down. See if there's anything in the paper yet."

He slowed the car. Mark twisted around to catch the headlines.

"Did you see anything?" Gary asked, picking up speed.

"Nothing. Guess we're not important enough."

They rode on in silence for a few blocks. Then Mark

spoke. His voice was so cold and emotionless, it took Gary a minute to grasp what was said.

"Gary, there's a car following us."

"A . . . what . . .?"

"It's the third car back. The gray one."

Gary glanced into the rear view mirror. "How do you know it's following us?"

"I noticed him slow down when we did back at the newsstand. I've been watching him ever since."

Carefully watching the third car, Gary slowed his speed. One car passed. The gray car slowed. Gary pushed down on the accelerator. The gap widened. Then the watched car picked up speed.

"You're right."

"Now what?"

"I'm going to try and lose him," Gary said. "In a couple of blocks I'll swing near Week's and drop you."

"I don't want to leave you," Mark protested.

"Don't be stupid," Gary said harshly. "There's no sense in us being picked up together."

Mark was silent.

At the next corner, Gary swung the car around and pushed the pedal to the floor. The car leaped forward. Mark twisted around to watch. Seconds passed. The street behind them remained empty. Maybe. . . . then the gray sedan turned in behind them.

"They're still on us, Gary."

Gary felt beads of sweat break out on his forehead as he pushed his car for more speed. Had they made a mistake? Were they going to get caught? Then he almost laughed. A few minutes before he had been thinking how nothing mattered anymore. Now he was worried about getting caught. So what if he did get caught? What difference did it make? So what! So what.

"I'm going to swing around this next corner and stop quick. Jump out and get out of sight."

Mark grabbed hold of the back of the seat to steady himself as Gary swung aound. He didn't have a chance to protest. Gary stopped and nearly pushed him out, then sped off.

Watching in the rear mirror, Gary saw Mark duck out of sight only seconds before the gray car came into sight. Gary knew escape was hopeless. He would lead the police on a few blocks to give Mark a chance, then he would stop. It really didn't matter.

John Fielding dropped his jacket in his bedroom, then continued on through the house in search of his mother. He needed someone to talk to. He found her in the kitchen, ironing her way through a stack of laundry. It wouldn't do any good to try and talk to her now, he decided. She didn't like to be disturbed when she was doing housework. He'd have to find someone else to talk to.

"Mom, is it all right if I call Jo Ann?"

"Yes," Marian Fielding answered her son without looking up from her work.

"Can I take the radio?"

"Yes, yes," Marian snapped. Why did the boy have to pester her when she was busy?

With lowered head, John shuffled into the kitchen to get the radio. Marian watched, but he didn't raise his head. There, she thought, she'd done it again. Without real reason she had snapped at him. True, it had been a rough day at the office. Then to come home to a messy house and a stack of ironing made it worse. And he always seemed to pick these times to pester.

They were poor excuses. It was wrong to yell at him. At times things got the best of her. Too much happening all at once. Poor John! He was at that awkward age. He didn't stop to think before he acted. Maybe if she and Ralph could find more time to spend with him.

If she could sit down and talk to John, he might end up seeing things a little more from her point of view. Maybe he would realize that the things he was pestering about weren't that important. One day he would ask her and Ralph to go to some football game, then they were needed to chaperon at a school dance. This was fine for parents who had the time, but with both her and Ralph working, time was at a premium.

John took the transistor radio off the shelf and started out of the kitchen. He hesitated, his mouth poised to speak, then turned away, leaving unsaid whatever thought was in his mind. Marian saw the gesture and read the hopelessness behind it. She couldn't be that bad.

"I'll never see how you can talk on the telephone with that thing plugged in your ear," she teased, trying to make up with him for being so grumpy.

A light flashed into his blue eyes. He laughed with instant spirit, the way he did when he considered her to be rather obsolete.

"It's hard for me to think without the radio," he explained for what he thought was the millionth time.

This Marian could easily believe. He had nearly driven both her and Ralph out of their minds with his constant playing of the radio, until they had thought up the ear plug arrangement.

"Don't talk too long," she called to him as he left the room. "Your father is going to call from the office. You know how upset he gets when the line is busy too long."

The smile faded from John's lips as quickly as it had appeared. He glanced back at his mother. She was busy with her ironing again. He turned away. It was always like this, he thought wistfully. A word or two were tossed in his direction, like a bone to a dog, then his parents drifted back to their own world. Who did they think they were trying to fool? He knew there was no room in their world for him.

Marian glanced up at the clock as she finished the shirt she was pressing. After six. How she hated it when Ralph had to work late. There was so little time when the three of them could be together. They were becoming strangers living in the same house.

This didn't seem to be the right way to raise a son. Marian wondered again if she should quit her job and stay at home. They no longer needed her income. Still . . . the idea of becoming a housewife after working so many years was repulsive. She enjoyed her job. Besides, she argued, John wasn't home much. And in another year they would need the money to put him through college.

That settled it. Things would go on as they had. Now if only John didn't talk on the telephone too long.

Jo Ann answered the telephone on the first ring. She had been expecting it. John always called the same time every night, even if he had just dropped her off home.

"Hi, Jo, what's doing?"

At his first greeting, Jo Ann smiled. She could picture him clearly in her mind, draped across a chair with the telephone receiver cradled against his shoulder. His free hand would be twisting the radio dial.

"Nothing much," she answered, "helping my mother with supper. I can talk for a few minutes."

"I have a great idea. It's getting dark out," he began in a conspiring voice, "why don't we sneak out and drive up to Miller's Creek?"

"Oh John, you're such a nut. You know full well that we'd both be scared stiff if we went there. You're so goofy I sometimes wonder why I go steady with you."

"It's because I'm so irresistible and you're madly in love with me," he answered cockily. Then in a lower, less confident voice, "even if I can't talk long. Dad's due to call home soon."

Those simple words seemed to shatter his carefree mood. Jo Ann sighed. There were times she felt sorry for John. His parents never seemed to include him in their lives. She was so close to her parents, it was hard to imagine what John felt. She knew he was unhappy at times.

"What are we going to do next Friday night?" she asked, to change the subject.

"Anything you like."

"My, you're agreeable. Yesterday you didn't seem too sure what you'd be doing."

He hesitated. "Well, everything worked out. I'm free to do whatever you'd like."

"Dotti still wants us to come to her party."

"Sounds fine to me," John answered. "Let's see, if I take mom to her bridge club . . . she can get a ride home . . . good, I can get a car. Let's plan on going. . . ."

Before he completed his sentence, a news bulletin broke into his thoughts.

". . . a suspect has been apprehended in the case involving the brutal murder of Harry Rosenthal outside his market early today. A witness reported seeing three young boys stage the holdup and shooting. Identity of the suspect is being withheld, but he is believed to be a local youth."

John yanked the radio plug from his ear. *Murder! Shot!* The two words whirled through his brain. It couldn't be the same. It was a coincidence. They had only knocked the old man down. How could they have shot anyone? They didn't have a gun. But still . . . it had to be the same. One caught . . . who?

"John . . .? Johnny, are you still there?"

He could hear Jo Ann through the whirling in his brain.

"A . . . yes . . . yes . . . oh, no!"

"John, what's wrong?"

Her concern snapped him from the daze. *Get hold of yourself. Make your plans.* But what? He still couldn't believe it had happened. What had gone wrong? He pressed a hand against his temple, trying to force his thoughts clear. *Murder!*

"Jo Ann . . . can you get out to meet me? In an hour?"

The desperate urgency in his voice frightened her. Something was wrong. "I don't know if I can," she said. "We're going to eat soon. I'll have to ask my mother."

"No!"

He answered so sharply, Jo Ann jumped. When his voice came over the line again it had dropped to a whisper. "I don't want anyone to know you're with me. I want you to come, but think of some other way to get out."

His request frightened her more. John never had asked

her to do anything like this before. What terrible thing had happened to make him do it now?

"All right, John, I'll meet you in the alley behind the drug store."

"Good," he whispered. "And Jo Ann . . . no matter what happens . . . remember . . . I love you."

His parting words were spoken so gently, it took her a moment to realize what he had actually said. What did he mean? "John. . . ."

There was no answer. He was gone.

An hour later Jo Ann found John waiting in the shadows behind the drug store. She smiled as he drove up to her, hoping the smile would hide her fear.

John stopped the car beside her. Instead of coming around and opening the car door as he usually did, he pushed it open from the inside. Jo Ann got in, pulling the door closed. Without speaking, John put the car into gear and drove off.

For several blocks, he crept along without headlights. Repeatedly he glanced into the rear view mirror. His every move seemed to speak of some terrible crisis.

Satisfied that no one was following, John switched on the headlights and picked up speed. Jo Ann waited for him to explain, as she knew he would — why he was driving through all the back streets — why they were heading out of town — why he was so jumpy.

Finally, when they passed beyond the outskirts of town, he spoke. "How did you get out?"

"I told mom I was going over to Dotti's to help with the party."

John nodded. He knew how hard it was for her to lie to her parents. It made him proud to know she cared for him that much, but at the same time it made him cringe to think he was pulling her down into the gutter with him.

"Maybe I should go by Dotti's for a minute later on," she added. "Then it wouldn't be an outright lie."

John didn't answer. He was so quiet. Jo Ann tried to

23

see his face in the lights of oncoming cars. He looked so distant and cold. What had happened? This was a John she didn't know.

A few miles out of town, he pulled off the highway into a deserted side road. He stopped the car and turned off the lights. The stillness of the night immediately surrounded them. The stars seemed to leap down from the sky. In the shrubs at the side of the road, the crickets resumed their chirping, unaware of the crisis going on nearby.

John turned to her. "Thanks for coming."

The suddenness of his voice startled her. "You sounded so worried on the phone . . . I thought . . . well . . . that something was wrong."

A long breath whistled between his lips. He turned back toward the steering wheel. Jo Ann was waiting for some kind of an explanation. She deserved at least that. He wanted to tell her. That's why he had brought her out here in the first place. But how could he begin? How did a guy tell his girl that he was a murderer?

"This isn't easy to talk about . . . especially to you." No, no, he thought, that's not what he meant. "What I mean, Jo Ann, is, it isn't very nice and I hate to have you hear it. Now that it's over . . . it seems like some terrible dream." His face twisted in pain as he struggled to put his feelings into words. "It's all so crazy and mixed up."

He fell silent again. Nervously, he rubbed his hands over the steering wheel making a funny squeaky noise. If only he could find the right words. Words that would make it easier for Jo Ann to accept and understand what had happened; understand his desperate feeling of nothingness. Did such words exist?

"I must talk to someone," he said hopelessly. No that again wasn't what he wanted to say. She wasn't just anyone. He wanted to talk to her and no one else, but he didn't want to involve her in something so terrible. Still, he needed her and in needing her he couldn't spare her. "I don't like involving you, Jo Ann . . . but . . . I need you.

There's no one else who can understand how I feel. No one else who cares like you do."

Jo Ann reached out and touched his arm. At first she had been frightened. Now she felt only his terrible need. "It's all right, John. I want to know everything you do. I don't want to be left out of any part of your life. No matter what it is, I'll understand. And it won't change anything between us."

Her words and the touch of her hand was the only encouragement John needed. "Did you hear the news tonight? About the holdup . . . and shooting?"

"Yes," she answered quietly. "Mother and I heard it while we were finishing dinner. She was upset when she heard that the one caught was a local boy." Jo Ann started to add that she had thought it terrible, but something stopped her. The fear grew in her again. Why had she stopped? What was it that she feared? What was John going to tell her?

"You know the boy the cops caught," John blurted out.

"Oh," she answered cautiously.

"It's Gary Wilson."

Jo Ann covered her mouth with her hands. How terrible! It couldn't be him. He was John's best friend.

"Is there some kind of a mistake?" she asked. It was hard to believe he would ever get involved in something like that.

Before John answered her question, he paused a long moment. The pause forewarned her that there had been no mistake. Gary was involved in the terrible crime. But there was more. A tightness grew in her chest. A shroud was hanging over her, ready to drop. She knew then . . . there was more . . . Gary was involved . . . but that wasn't all. Something was reaching out for her John. Then he said it and all doubts vanished, stealing any last small ray of hope.

"His arrest was no mistake, Jo Ann. He had a part in the robbery. I know. . . . I was there, too."

These were the words she had fearfully expected, but

25

still they came as a shock. She wanted to cover her ears and scream no, no, no! This wasn't real. It couldn't be happening. Not John! Not her John!

The horror of the terrible reality began seeping through her unreceptive mind. She pressed her lips tightly together hoping it would end; praying for it to go away; knowing it was real. Why, oh, why, had it happened?

"Jo Ann?"

The voice intruding into her thoughts shook her. It wasn't John's voice. It was the voice of a little boy pleading for understanding — for acceptance — for help. John needed her. What could she do? What had happened was awful. A man was dead, and there was no way she could erase it. It was too late.

She closed her eyes, trying to delay the decision. Without question, John had done wrong. No matter how small his part had been, he was still wrong. He should go to the police. She should tell him this. Something else entered in. She was in love with John. They had planned to live their lives together — such a wonderful life. Could one mistake, regardless how terrible, end all this? She and John were young. They had so much time before them. Could it all end in one day?

John was waiting for her answer. She knew he would never ask her to do anything. The decision had to be completely hers. He needed her. She couldn't let him down Digging her fingernails into the palms of her hands to steady her voice, Jo Ann answered.

"I'm all right, John. I love you."

The assurance of her words brought immediate relief. His shoulders sank back against the seat. "It isn't fair to involve you," he said quietly. "I hadn't planned to. I didn't think it would end this way."

Enough, enough, Jo Ann wanted to cry. She didn't want to hear anymore. It would be easier if she didn't know all that had happened. Then she could cling to John and forget the past. But that wouldn't help John. He needed someone to talk to. She couldn't fail him.

"John, I think it would be easier if you told me what happened," she forced herself to say.

He gripped the steering wheel tightly. It was time. He had to begin. He had brought her out here to tell her what had happened. How was he to begin? How did you tell someone you loved that there was no reason for what you had done? The whole thing had just happened. Your only excuse was the terrible feeling of emptiness; a feeling that nothing mattered any more; life had lost all meaning and desire for him? Could she ever understand, that for a time the love they shared and the life they had planned together lost all importance? Could he expect her love to survive this?

He leaned his head against the side window and took a deep breath. Slowly he exhaled, delaying the beginning a moment longer.

"It doesn't seem real anymore," he began, "even though it just happened this morning. It seems like a dream or a story I heard. I don't even know how it happened. It just did."

Slowly, with growing pain, the tale unwound. The plans made in fun, to be doing something. The half jesting idea that they really try and pull it off. The detailed arrangements. The action . . . the action that had carried them farther than they had ever dreamed.

"None of us knew the old man had even been hurt. We were running back to the car. The old guy must have wiggled out of the ropes we tied him with. He came after us waving a gun. Mark made a dive for him. I was getting into the car. I went to help Mark and we all fell to the sidewalk. I heard some noise . . . but Gary was gunning the car so I thought it was that. When the old man didn't get up . . . I thought Mark had knocked him out."

The story ended. That was all there was to it.

Jo Ann remained quiet for a long minute. Now that the suspense was over and she had heard the whole story, the shock lessened. Crime itself didn't shock her. She had been raised in a generation of crime and violence. The idea that John might be connected with it had been the shock. Now that she knew the worst of it, she could turn her attention to the future. What should they do now?

"Have you said anything to your parents?"

His answer was prefaced by a sharp, sarcastic laugh. "No, they wouldn't have time to listen."

"What do you plan?"

"I . . ." He shook his head. "I don't know, Jo Ann. Our thinking ended with the robbery. We made plans in case anyone was caught because it was part of the game."

Jo Ann's question forced John to think hard. They weren't a gang of kids making silly plans. They now were criminals. It was over, and nothing would put things back the way they had been. A man had been murdered. He was dead. He wasn't going to come back. In those few, short minutes, all their lives had been changed.

At the time of planning, the outcome hadn't seemed to matter. Now . . . he was beginning to wonder . . . maybe it did matter. There were a few things he held important; his love for Jo Ann and his freedom. He hadn't thought about losing them. Now they were threatened. What could he do? Was it too late to think about it? No, it couldn't be! Please, God don't let it be too late!

John stopped. It did matter. Something mattered. He didn't want to lose what he had. What could he do to save it now? If he had only felt this before.

"John . . . what were the plans you made in case someone was caught?"

She knew what the answer had to be. The only thing left for them to do was run away. Up until now they had been average kids. They obeyed laws and stayed out of trouble. This was all going to change. Jo Ann had no illusions. Once the decision was made and they started to run, they would be running the rest of their lives.

If they stayed, it would be years and years before they could be together again. John could even be sent to jail for life. No, she wouldn't think of that. They would leave.

John began to answer her question. "If anyone was

28

caught . . . the others were to go to where we hid the money, split it up and leave. That's . . . that's the part I couldn't do," he added quickly. "I couldn't leave you."

He reached out and took her hand. They were so young to be making such decisions. They looked at one another. The night was dark, yet they could see. At this moment they were closer than ever before. Without speaking, they were sharing the same thoughts. Their lives were committed to one another.

"John . . . if you want me . . . I'll go with you."

"Would you really?" he asked in wonder. This was what he wanted most of all. He had longed to ask her, but feared having her give up so much.

The wonder Jo Ann heard in his voice made her realize what she was really doing. Before, she had thought out what it would cost them. Now she had to consider what it would cost her. She was going to leave her family. Chances were slim she'd ever see any of them again. A life away from all she had known was hard to imagine, but a life away from John and the love she now felt for him was harder to imagine. If the choice had to be made, there was only one thing she could do.

"John, all I want is to be with you. If it means leaving, I'm ready to go. Without you, life doesn't exist."

So this was love. The word suddenly blazed with new meaning as John realized what Jo Ann was willing to do for him Could he let her do it? More than anything else he wanted to go away with her. Away anywhere. Away and erase the memory of all that had happened this day. The aimlessness vanished. A life with Jo Ann was important.

"Are you sure this is what you want?" he forced himself to say in one last attempt to dissuade her. "Are you sure you'll be happy with me as your husband? Knowing what I've done?"

"Once we've gone, John, we'll never talk about this again. We've discussed it here. When we leave, we'll leave it here."

"Shall we go?"

"Yes. Let's go right now. Let's leave without going back at all."

Quickly, her mind whispered, *quickly before we change our minds.*

Mark Hayden parked his car in the garage. He sat there a moment to think. The news bulletin had been clear. Gary had been caught. What had gone wrong? And the old man? How had that happened? Gary was in jail. Mark knew what he had to do. First he would talk to his father, then he would go.

Felix Hayden was in his study, bent over a stack of papers. Mark hesitated at the half-open door. His father hated to be interrupted while he was working. Tonight was different. Mark felt this interruption was warranted.

He knocked on the solid oak door, then stepped into the room. "Dad, may I talk to you?"

Felix looked up with a frown. "Is it important?"

"If it wasn't important, Sir, I'd know better than to interrupt."

There was a trace of insolence in the boy's answer. Felix chuckled. He admired any person who'd stand up to him. Mark especially. Someday Mark would be taking over the empire Felix was building for him. He needed to know how to stand up to people.

"All right, sit down. I can spare a few minutes."

Felix watched his son cross the room with determined steps. He caught the way Mark sat in the chair and tried to lean back with a relaxed appearance. The boy was nervous but determined.

"Well . . . what is it?"

Mark drew a deep breath, ready to begin. He had to come right to the point and speak with assurance if he was going to influence his father. Felix had a way of confusing the facts. This time it wasn't going to happen.

"Did you hear about the robbery and killing across town today?"

Felix nodded. "On the way home from the plant."

30

"The police caught one of the suspects."

Again Felix nodded but didn't speak. He began chewing on the end of the cigar protruding from his lips. He was guessing at what his son wanted, and began planning his own answer.

"Gary Wilson was the one they picked up."

This was a surprise to Felix. "Doris Wilson's son?" Felix chuckled. There was a woman who knew what she wanted and usually got it. "I'm surprised she allowed Gary to get caught. Bet right now she's after some senator to get him off."

Felix laughed at his own joke. Mark smiled weakly.

"Well, that's something," Felix said. "Did you know anything about it?"

The question was meant to catch Mark off guard and it did. He wanted to approach the subject more subtly. "Yes, Sir, I knew all about the robbery. I was in on the planning. I think I'm the one who killed the old man."

Whatever Felix had anticipated from his son, it nowhere near reached the magnitude of Mark's actual confession. The cigar dropping to the corner of his mouth was the only outward display of emotion, but inwardly, Felix's thoughts were tumbling.

Ages of time seemed to pass while Mark waited for his father to speak. He knew there would be no show of temper, no loud shouting. His father employed those means only when he knew it would achieve a purpose. Something else was coming.

Mark glanced around nervously. Felix quietly chewed on the end of his cigar. Mark was sure he was considering all the angles and all the possibilities. Then he would come out with a plan of action. This was the way he did everything — cold and calculating, even murder. Just once . . . if only he would be different . . . if only. . . . But that was foolishness, Mark knew.

This time it didn't matter. This time Mark had a plan of his own and he intended to carry it out. Somehow

31

he had to prove he was a man capable of following his own plan.

"When exactly did this happen?" Felix asked, breaking the silence.

"This morning."

The battle of wits began.

"How did Wilson get caught?"

"I don't know. We were being followed. He let me out and went on."

"Were you all together?"

"We went together in Gary's car. Later he dropped John off, then me."

"They probably traced the car," Felix thought out loud. "Will the others squeal on you?"

"No!"

Mark's answer was instant in defense of his friends. Then his thoughts sharpened. What was his father looking for? Mark wished he hadn't been so spontaneous in his answer. It could have been an effective stalling device if his father pushed too hard.

"Good," Felix said, getting to his feet. "Now we have to make some plans."

His father seemed so calm that Mark wondered if he really understood that a man was dead. The time to exert himself was now, before his father got too wrapped up in other plans.

"Dad, I already know what I'm going to do. I've thought about it, and I've decided the best thing is to give myself up. I'm going down to the police station."

"Why?"

Mark had prepared himself for a lengthy argument from his father, not a fast question. Mark looked at him. Surely he was going to ask more. Not just why. Felix asked no more. Why? Well, because. It was the only right thing to do.

"Why are you going to run down and give yourself up?" Felix asked again.

Mark's face twisted in confusion. What was his father

after? His lips quivered as he tried to form his thoughts. All his preplanning was gone.

"I . . . I want to go . . . well, because it's what I should do. I'm more guilty than the others."

"Rubbish! That's a lot of foolish sentiment."

Mark was stunned. What did his father mean? Surely he didn't mean to defy the law? "Dad, I did it," he pleaded. "I want to turn myself in."

"Now you listen to what I want," Felix said, towering over his son. "You're not going to do anything until we've made some kind of plans. If you went storming down to the jail tonight, they'd lock you up and that would end it. Let's sit still and think this out a bit."

His father's overpowering will was descending fast. Mark struggled against it. "I have thought it out," he insisted. "I want to go now. I killed him. I don't want anyone else taking the blame for me."

As Mark grew excited, his father got over his first shock and grew calmer. "What you did was terrible. I don't understand how you could have gotten involved, but you killed a man. It's going to take a lot of planning and resourcefulness to get you out of this. We can't undo what's done, but we can try to keep it from ruining your life."

Mark stared at the big man. He was crushed. He couldn't believe his father would really defy the law. Yet no matter how he looked at it, this was the only conclusion he could draw. His father was handling this the same way he handled everything else — twisting, turning and hiding.

In a casual way, Felix closely watched his son. What Mark told him had been a greater shock than he wanted to admit. It was a stupid act, and Mark wasn't a stupid boy. Luckily, Felix had been able to keep his head. It had been frightening to see the possibility of all his work sliding down the drain. He had built the business for Mark and he wasn't going to let it be thrown away.

First of all, he had to crush Mark's idea of giving himself up. Time was needed to do a little planning.

Pressure had never worked with Mark. Appealing to his senses was the best way to handle him.

"Mark, I don't think you quite understood what I meant," Felix began. "I know how you feel. Your reaction was a normal one. I feel we should talk more before rushing into action."

As he spoke, Felix watched for Mark's reaction. Mark was quiet, but he didn't seem to be agreeing. "Let's see if I can get the facts together," Felix said, stalling for time. "The shooting was an accident?"

"Yes, Sir. He came after us with a gun. He took us by surprise. There was a fight . . . well, I guess he was shot. I didn't even know the gun had gone off."

"If it happened that way, we have some hope. We can get the company lawyer over here. You tell him exactly what happened and see what he can suggest. Maybe we can say it was a club initiation or something like that."

While he talked, Felix slowly made his way across the room toward the oak door. There was only one way he knew to handle Mark now. He would have to keep the boy from doing anything.

"I'll call Larry and get him over here right away. He's a good lawyer. It will only take a few minutes. Then, if you still want to go ahead with your idea, you can. Besides, your friends won't know if you get there tonight or tomorrow."

The net was being drawn closer. Mark could feel his father's will swaying his own. This time . . . this once . . . Mark wanted to carry out his own plans. He was tired of having everything planned for him; of being told just what he had to do. This time he was right. He had been so sure his father would agree. The business, his future, nothing else mattered. There was one thing he had to do; give himself up and he was going to do it.

"Dad, I don't want to wait and talk to Larry. I want . . ."

His words and decision came too late. As he turned to speak, his father stepped out through the door and

34

pulled it closed behind him. There was a single click as the key turned in the lock.

He was betrayed. Bolting up, he dashed to the door, pounding his fists against it. All the time he had thought his father was trying to help him, he was planning this. He should have known.

"You lied!" he screamed through the locked door. "Let me out! Open the door!"

His father's voice came through the door, cold and cruel. "You just sit down and cool off. I'm going to talk to Larry. Maybe he can find a way to get you stupid kids out of trouble. When I come back I'll let you out."

"But I've a right to do what. . . ."

"You don't have any rights left," his father outshouted him in his first display of emotion. "You're a thief and a murderer!"

The anger and bitterness in his father's voice kept Mark from saying anything further. It was useless. His father was disappointed in him. Or, was he disappointed in the fact that all the plans he had made for Mark were now ending?

Mark leaned his forehead against the door. Tears filled his eyes. He had planned it out so carefully. It was right, and he wanted to do it. His father was no angel. In the past Mark had learned of certain business deals his father had been connected with. There were a few Mark was sure he wouldn't want spread around town, but his father had always insisted this was different. It was business.

Business, Felix had taught his son, was handled differently than personal matters. There were times when an honest man had to lie and cheat a little. Mark had tried to accept this. Now his father was using the same manipulation in his private life. It didn't seem to be any different after all. Just once, couldn't his father be honest?

Back and forth across the room Mark paced. He had to get out. Somehow he had to find a way. He pried his mind for some key. His mother and sisters were away. Had they been home, Mark doubted they would have gone against his father. He hammered at the door again. It was solid. A chair wouldn't make the slightest dent.

There was one large window, twelve feet above the ground. It didn't open, and the panes were too small for Mark to fit through. The room was escape proof. There wasn't even an extension telephone because his father didn't like being disturbed at work.

Crossing to the window, Mark stared out into the falling darkness. Absently he ran his fingers along the window panes. The glass was smooth and cool to touch. He had to get out. There had to be a way.

His fingers stopped. Something caught his attention. It was a mar in the glass — a slight raise breaking the smoothness. He looked to see. It was the magnetic tape connected to the burglar system. If it was broken, the whole system went off drawing every cop in the neighborhood.

The tape! That was it. This was his escape. Mark grabbed a paperweight from the desk. With careful aim, he threw it through the window, giving little thought to the fact that he was also throwing away his freedom and his life.

The car came slowly down the street, passed the police station, then stopped a short distance from the entrance. A young boy got out. His companion slid across into the driver's seat.

"Now you know what to do?"

She nodded. He knew it was a needless question. They had just spent the last half hour making their plans. He didn't know what else to say. He didn't want this moment to end, but he couldn't think of any way to prolong it.

These same thoughts were running through Jo Ann's mind. She wanted to be sure that he knew what she felt. This was the only way it could end. They had tried, but running away wouldn't solve anything. Why, oh, why, did it have to happen to them?

"John . . . I'm glad we came back. I know it will work out."

He forced a smile on his lips. Now that they were here, he wished they were still out on the highway. The idea of returning seemed big and noble out there. Here, it seemed empty and meaningless.

He loved Jo Ann. This was the only thing important to him; the only thing he could rely on. There was still time to go. They could leave, lose their identities and start their lives over again. All he had to do was get back into the car. Jo Ann would understand. What was right? In the whole mixed up world, what was right?

John leaned through the open window. For one last, long, minute he looked at her. He kissed her gently. How long would this kiss have to last? A crushing ache gripped his heart. How could he leave her? How had he ever gotten involved in such a deed?

"Be easy with my folks, Jo Ann," he said stepping back quickly. "And don't forget . . . I love you."

Jo Ann nodded, not trusting herself to speak. She watched him walk away. A great part of her life went with him. Moments they had spent together flashed through her mind. They were happy, carefree moments. It hurt to know that these moments had come to an end. Nothing would ever again be the same. Squaring his shoulders, John marched toward the police station. Jo Ann started the car. The sound brought a tightness to his chest, but he didn't slow his step or turn. She was leaving, but he could hold to the love they shared. He had that.

As he reached the station door, a patrol car drew up. A policeman jumped out, then helped a handcuffed prisoner from the back seat.

"Hello, Mark," John greeted, not at all surprised to see his friend.

"Hi, John," the handcuffed prisoner answered.

Together they entered the station.

CHAPTER THREE

Doris Wilson had been spending one of her infrequent nights at home when the police called. At first Doris thought it was a joke. Sometimes her son Gary played little jokes on her. Not this time. The man on the phone assured her that he was a police officer and her son was being held. He explained what had happened and what should be done. She heard the words, but the meaning didn't register. Gary was in jail. This was all she understood.

For over an hour she sat frozen in the chair. It couldn't be — not Gary — not her son, but it was true.

As the first shock wore off, her thinking cleared. Plans started creeping into her mind. She had to get Gary out of jail. How could she do it? She needed help. One by one she thought of the men she knew. Which of them would help her? Which of them could she force to help her? It didn't matter what she had to do or who she had to hurt, but she had to get Gary out of jail. That was all that mattered.

Judge Bernie Nelson reached the courthouse much earlier than usual. The halls were silent. He needed the silence to think. He had to make a decision. It was a troublesome decision no matter which side he took.

Nelson sat at his desk. The only object to mar the uniform neatness of the desk was the telephone. It had all started with that ugly, black telephone. He felt like flinging it across the room. How foolish! Smashing it wouldn't erase his problem. There was only one way to really erase it, and that was against the law.

The night before he had been working late. The telephone rang and he'd answered. It hadn't taken long for him to recognize the voice at the other end. It was Doris Wilson. He had almost forgotten her. If only she had forgotten him and gone on to other prey. What a foolish dream. Women like her never freed their prey.

The call had been short. Doris had been very upset. Her son was being held on a charge of murder. She had to get him out of jail. Nelson, being a judge, was the most logical one to turn to for help.

No mention was made of the party or the ride home afterward, but that wasn't necessary. The judge knew she wouldn't hesitate to use the incident, innocent though it was, to gain her end.

After calming her down, he told her to get some sleep because there was nothing to be done that evening. He would check into it and call her back in the morning.

There was no use delaying any longer. Slowly he dialed the number. She answered on the first ring.

"Oh, Judge, I'm so glad you called. I hate having to bother you this way, but I'm so terribly upset, and I don't know what to do."

"That's all right, Doris, I can understand."

"It's hard to be patient and wait, knowing Gary's in jail."

"I appreciate your anxiety." He tried to sound sympathetic, and yet businesslike. "First, you'll need a good lawyer. The best one in town is Grant Williams. If I talk to him he will help us get someone good."

The name was well-known to Doris. "If he's the best, why don't we get him?"

"Well . . . I don't think he'll take it. He's a very busy man," Nelson stuttered.

"Do you know him?"

"Why, yes. His father and I were good friends." Judge

Nelson regretted his words as soon as he spoke. He foresaw her next request, and he wouldn't dare deny it.

"Would you call him and get an appointment for me? I'll ask him myself to defend Gary."

This was less than Nelson had expected. He quickly agreed. Doris thanked him and hung up.

She sounded so sweet and sincere. Nelson wondered how much it would take to change her attitude. If he had refused to help her, he little doubted what she would have done.

Doris sat at the telephone for a few minutes and thought over what the judge had said. If Grant Williams was the best, she wouldn't settle for anyone else. Somehow she would make him take the case. First, she needed an opening. Judge Nelson would take care of that.

Next, she had to find out a bit more about this Grant Williams. Then she would decide the best way to handle him. There was always a way. He would be her means of getting Gary out of jail.

The office of Grant Williams was located in the downtown section of the city. It occupied a large suite on the second floor of the building. The spaciousness of his suite, the decor of the office and the ability of his private secretary showed his success.

Grant entered the building. Pausing in front of the newsrack, he fumbled in his pocket for a dime. Before he dropped it in the slot, he saw the rack was empty. That was funny. He had never found it empty at this time of the morning. Probably someone forgot to fill it.

He turned and headed toward the coffee shop. At the door he again stopped. The place was packed. All his colleagues were there, and they all had newspapers spread in front of them. The headlines stood out:

BRUTAL MURDER ON SOUTH SIDE

Discussing a murder over coffee wasn't Grant's way of starting the day. He fled upstairs to his office.

Louise looked up from her typewriter when Grant entered. "Good morning. You're in a little early."

"Didn't stop for coffee," he explained. "The shop was packed, and everyone had a paper in front of him. I'm sure they're all talking about the murder."

Louise made a face. "Wasn't it terrible."

"Maybe I'll take a look at your paper later on. Right now I want to get to work."

"I'll have some coffee brought up," Louise said, anticipating his wishes. "By then these letters will be ready to sign."

"Good."

Grant went into his office. Louise followed him with her eyes until the door shut. What a nice day this was going to be. She sighed and smiled. Would she ever get over the sudden joy of seeing him each morning? It was ten years now, and she still felt the same.

Grant had barely started working when the telephone rang. The button over his private line blinked. Only personal calls came in over this line. He answered it before Louise picked it up.

"Hello, Grant, this is Bernie Nelson. Am I interrupting anything?"

"No, Judge, not at all."

"I won't take much of your time," Nelson promised. "Have you seen the headlines in this morning's paper?"

"If you mean the murder, I heard a little on the radio."

"It's going to be a nasty case," Nelson continued. "Terrible shame. Bad for the city."

For a few minutes they talked about the growing juvenile problem. "This is different from the normal run of juvenile cases," Nelson said emphatically. "This one is going to involve some leading citizens in the city. And since you haven't seen the paper, you don't know but it's already tried and convicted the boys."

Grant didn't answer or argue with his friend. He had

the feeling that Nelson had something more on his mind. The judge wasn't a man who called just to chat.

"Well, to get to the point. I know what a busy man you are, Grant, but I'd like to ask a favor of you."

Without hesitation, Grant agreed to any favor.

"I believe you're going to be asked to defend these boys. I'd appreciate it if you'd listen to the offer and give it serious consideration."

Grant was surprised by the request. There wasn't anything really wrong with a judge asking a lawyer to take a certain case. It just wasn't like Judge Nelson to do it. What had made him act like this now?

"It's a tragic affair," the judge continued, wanting to further explain himself. "The way the newspaper is distorting the story, it's going to take a strong man to see those boys get a fair trial. I don't know anyone else capable of the job."

An awkward silence fell between them. Judge Nelson was embarrassed for what he had been compelled to say. Grant didn't know how to answer. This wasn't at all like his old friend.

"I'll try to do what I can," Grant finally replied.

"Good," Nelson said with relief. "I was sure you would. And Grant . . . thanks."

"That's okay, Judge."

Nelson hung up, leaving a very puzzled lawyer at the other end of the line. He hadn't agreed to do anything, and yet the judge was happy. What was it all about?

As soon as Judge Nelson called and said Williams would talk to her, Doris had started to work. She had found out a few things about this lawyer and knew how she was going to handle him. He was a bachelor who appreciated certain things. She was determined to add herself to his list if it would help get Gary out of jail.

Doris entered Grant's office and walked briskly to the secretary's desk. "I'm Doris Wilson, and I'd like to see Mr. Williams," she announced.

The arrogance and authority in the woman's voice created an immediate dislike in Louise. She looked up to see who had come barging in, demanding such immediate attention.

"Did you want to make an appointment?" Louise asked, trying to overcome the instant dislike.

"No," Doris answered briskly. "I'd like to see him right now, please."

"I'm very sorry, but his schedule is full today."

"Please tell him that I'm here. He'll see me."

The two women glared at one another.

"If you'll sit down, I'll check with him," Louise finally said.

Doris flashed a sickly sweet smile, but remained standing. Louise delayed as long as she could, then picked up a stack of letters and went into Grant's office, carefully shutting the door behind her.

Grant glanced up as she came in. "Done already?"

"With most of them."

The tone in her voice gave away her irritation. Grant looked closer. "What's the matter?"

"A woman just came barging in here, demanding to see you and refusing to wait. Maybe I'm getting old and grouchy, but she really irked me."

"I don't think you're a bit old and grouchy. Your judgment is good enough for me. What did the woman want?"

Louise quickly told him of Doris Wilson and her demands. Grant was about to have Louise turn the woman away, when a suspicion entered his mind. There was something familiar about the name Wilson. He glanced at the morning paper Louise had laid on his desk. Wilson was the name of one of the boys involved in the murder. The pieces began to fall into place. Someone wasn't wasting any time. He had just finished talking to the judge — now the visit. What was the connection between this woman and his old friend? Was this the motive for Nelson's unusual behavior? Grant wanted to find out.

"Ask her to come in."

Louise jerked her head in surprise.

"I'm sorry, I forgot to tell you she was coming," he hastily added to explain.

Without answering, Louise left the room. She was hurt. Grant reproved himself for being so thoughtless. He fully expected to talk to the woman and have her on her way in short order. Then they could forget all about it. All he really wanted to do was satisfy his curiosity. He didn't know Doris Wilson.

The door opened and she stepped into the room. Her unannounced appearance caught Grant unprepared. He stood up quickly, trying to cover his surprise, and stumbled over his feet.

She watched him, the trace of a smile crossing her lips. It made him feel very foolish.

"Good morning, Mrs. Wilson. Do sit down," he said, trying to regain his composure.

"Good morning, Mr. Williams. It's good of you to see me so quickly."

Doris crossed the room to the chair in front of the desk. Grant used the moment to observe her. She was well-dressed, distinguished looking with a confident bearing. This was hardly the matronly mother of a teenage boy he was expecting. He could understand Nelson's attraction. What was the extent of the connection between them?

Doris sat in the chair and arranged her skirt. She looked up suddenly and squarely met his eyes. A teasing smile told him that she was quite aware of his appraisal and also confident of the outcome.

"Judge Nelson called and said I might be of some assistance to you," Grant said, sitting down. This wasn't what he had planned to say. He was leaving himself open for a request for help. What was so distracting him?

"He told me that he had," Doris replied. "It was very dear of him to help me. I was so upset . . . he took over and told me exactly what to do."

Her sentence ended with a catch in her voice. It reminded Grant that she was a mother and her son was being held for murder.

"I know you're very busy, Mr. Williams, so I'll come right to the point. The charges against my son and the other boys are very serious. I want the best legal assistance for Gary. When Judge Nelson told me you were the best, I came right over."

"There are many fine attorneys capable of handling this for you," Grant argued weakly. How hard it was to resist this woman.

"You're being modest. Many people have mentioned your abilities. You're the man we need. You see, Mr. Williams, I'm not just another anxious parent trying to get a son out of trouble. This case is different."

The same words again. Grant listened quietly.

"Regardless of what the newspaper reported," Doris continued, "the boys are not bad boys. They have no police records. Their school reports are excellent. I've raised Gary by myself, and he's never given me a bit of trouble. He doesn't deserve to be sent to prison for one mistake."

"If the newspaper accounts are at all factual, the boys have confessed to the crime. There's not much that can be done in a case like this," Grant pointed out.

Doris had a ready answer for his objection. "They have admitted partial guilt, but the police and papers are building it all out of proportion. They're trying to make the boys pay for all the delinquency that's gone on lately. They'll be punished more than they deserve."

Her arguments were simple, logical and very effective. Despite his predetermined feelings, Grant felt himself swaying. She had some good points. This woman seemed to know exactly how to reach him. Each time he spoke, he seemed to give in a little more to her.

"I can understand your concern, Mrs. Wilson, especially in the way the story is building up. I really don't have much free time, but I will go talk to the boys and see if I can help them. If I don't feel I can handle the case, I will find a good lawyer for you."

"That's all I can ask," she replied.

Without intending it, Grant had practically agreed to take the case. He caught a note of triumph in her voice. What was the battle that she felt she had won?

"As far as the fee is concerned . . ."

A protest rose instantly to Grant's lips. Surely the woman didn't think that money was the cause of his hesitations. Before he spoke, he met her eyes. That wasn't the point she was making at all, and his jumping to conclusions amused her.

". . . I believe we can work out a satisfactory arrangement," Doris continued. "I've talked to the Fieldings. We've agreed to ask you to represent the boys jointly. I'm sure Felix Hayden will join us. He's not a man to settle for less than the best."

Her words were a simple statement with no flattery attached. Again she had made her point, and he was left without a reply.

"I will see the boys. This case is different from the kind I normally handle. After I see them I will call you."

"All right, Mr. Williams, I'll wait to hear from you."

After she had left, Grant sat at his desk thinking. What an unusual morning. First the judge's call, and then the Wilson woman. He still wondered what her connection was with the judge. She was . . . so different. Was she after her son's release . . . or did she have something else in mind? For some reason, Grant had a strange feeling about her. And the boys in jail . . . how guilty were they? Why had they done it? Were the newspapers completely out of line? His curiosity was aroused. Was it the case or the woman?

With a sigh, Grant leaned forward in his chair. He was getting nothing accomplished. He couldn't concentrate on the paper work. He might as well talk to the boys. Reaching across the desk, he flipped the button on the intercom.

"Louise, I'm going down to the jail and talk to those boys connected with the murder. Hold all my calls."

Before she could raise any question, the line went dead. Louise spat out a long breath. It was that Wilson woman. First of all, he had spent half the morning with her, and now he was running out to work on the case and neglecting the important work he had left in the office.

In spite of her efforts, Louise could feel the jealousy mounting. She had no right to such feelings. Grant was a bachelor. She certainly had no ties to him. It was just that she didn't trust that woman. Maybe it was jealousy, but Louise was sure that woman was after more than she admitted.

CHAPTER FOUR

THE DAY WAS nearly over when Grant returned to his office. He had gone to the jail seeking answers for two questions: what the boys had actually done, and why they had done it. He came back with neither answer.

The newspaper claimed the boys were cold-blooded killers deserving the maximum penalty. After talking to them, Grant felt different. The boys were shocked by the murder. They couldn't explain how it happened. Not only that, but they couldn't explain why it happened. They couldn't give Grant any kind of a motive.

These two things were bad enough, but what disturbed Grant the most was the fact that they didn't seem to care what happened to them because of the crime. They were unconcerned about their whole future.

Louise was locking her desk for the night when Grant walked in. He was surprised to see her. "You're working late, aren't you?"

"I wanted to finish a few things. I'll take a long lunch tomorrow," she promised. "You sound tired."

Her words stopped him. Was he tired? Yes, but it was more a mental weariness. What he had found in talking to the boys confused and upset him.

"I don't mind staying a little longer," Louise offered.

He started to protest, then stopped and grinned. "You're reading my thoughts again. I would appreciate it if you'd take a few notes for me while they're fresh in my mind."

She took out a pad and pencil. Grant sat down on the

edge of the desk and stared out the window at the darkening city. A long moment passed before he spoke. Why, why, why? The question slapped at him from every direction. Why had it happened? Why had they done it? Why didn't they care?

"Louise, this case is baffling me, and I've hardly gotten into it. The law is cold sometimes. Everything is black or white. When something gray comes along, it confuses everyone."

Louise listened to him, but her sympathies weren't with the case. This was one she wished he wouldn't take. She had a feeling that it was going to mean trouble. Anything concerning that Wilson woman meant trouble.

"There was such a conflict in stories, I decided to talk to the boys firsthand."

He got up and stood by the window. This story was happening right here — to him, not in New York or Los Angeles, but right here.

"I talked to each of the boys, but I only understood half of what they told me. Their reasoning and thinking is far from mine. We're very different. Still . . . I like them. They seem like nice kids."

"Nice kids don't murder helpless old men," Louise shot back.

"Up to now," Grant answered, "up to now. But we might be witnessing the beginning of a change. I suppose it's the implication that really worries me. They each admit taking part in the crime, but they can't explain why."

"Or wouldn't," Louise said sarcastically.

Grant was so absorbed in his thoughts, he didn't notice her acid remark. "They're not rebels out against anything. They didn't do it for kicks. To them it just happend — almost without them knowing it."

"Grant, you're not making sense. The whole crime was carried out with too much precision to have just happened."

He dropped his arms to his side in a gesture of dismay. Of course he knew he wasn't making sense. It couldn't just have happened. The boys had even admitted planning the robbery.

"You're right, Louise, I'm not making sense. I can't seem to. What I've learned . . . well, this case is different from any I've started before. I've got a feeling a good many ideas are going to be changed by it."

"Maybe you shouldn't take it," she suggested hopefully.

He shook his head. "No, I think I should. I think I can help these boys. But first I have to understand them. We're years apart on that score."

If he insisted on taking the case, Louise decided she had better help him. "Why don't you have a talk with Reverend Lowell. He used to work at a youth center before he came here."

"Hey! that's right. He could probably explain what these kids mean by 'nothingness'." Grant glanced at the calendar. "We have a lunch appointment tomorrow. I'll talk to him then."

Wednesday noon, Grant was walking down the block to meet his friend for lunch. As he walked he mentally formed the questions he wanted to ask Judd. There had been times before he'd ask Judd questions, but the minister hadn't known the answers. Maybe today Judd's God would be listening better.

The weekly luncheons dated back to the time Judd moved to the city as the new pastor of the large Grace Brethren Church. There were no two more unlikely men to become fast friends. Grant wasn't against religion. It had its place, it was just that he didn't need it.

After analyzing their friendship over a period of time, Grant concluded that basically they were alike. They both had dedicated their lives to the pursuit of their work. Grant believed law and order had the answer to all problems; Judd believed his Christ had all the answers.

"Hey, Grant!"

The loud hail halted Grant. Judd was coming up the street behind him, a wide grin spread all over his face.

The grin plus the sandy hair falling in his eyes gave the minister a collegian look.

"Say, you're in quite a serious mood," Judd said as he drew abreast. "What fair lady dominates the thoughts of our city's most eligible bachelor?"

"Unfortunately, it's not a lady. It's the Rosenthal case," Grant admitted.

"Are you going to take it?" Judd asked.

"I'm not sure yet."

"You will," Judd said positively.

"You're probably right," he admitted.

They continued on to the restaurant. While they waited for their food, Grant brought up his question. "Judd, you've worked with kids far more than I have. Maybe you can help me."

"I'll try," Judd agreed, wondering what impossible question Grant would ask him today.

"I went to talk to the boys," Grant began. "I found I couldn't understand them. Their reasoning or thinking seemed so different from mine. Their sense of values were different."

"They are different," Judd said. "They are a new breed — different from any previous generation. But we made them that way — too much crime, sex, bombs and wars."

"Anyway, the one thing that really bothers me is their attitude. They admit they're guilty, but not one of them can tell me why he took part in the crime. The papers have labeled the shooting a crime without motive. I don't think this is true. They had some reason — the thing is to find it."

"Couldn't they give you any idea what it was?"

Grant shook his head. "The only answer I get is, 'It just seemed to happen.' I've eliminated money, thrill, grudge and a dare. Where do I go from here? You've worked with boys. Why do such outstanding boys get involved in such a crime?"

Judd didn't have the answer. Grant had done it again.

Judd sometimes got the feeling Grant expected him to call down some mystical power from above to get answers. Of course he couldn't do that. Christ had all the answers, but Judd had to seek them through prayer, not the waving of a wand. Just once, though, Judd wished he could give Grant a direct answer when he asked a question. Maybe this way he could prove to the lawyer the power of God.

"I don't know where you're going to find the motives of these boys. With the slum kids it was easy. It usually was hunger. Your boys have a much deeper problem. I doubt if I'd understand them any better than you."

Grant nodded. He hadn't really expected Judd to be able to help him. He never had before. "Well, somewhere I have to find it."

When Grant returned from lunch, he was deep in thought. In one of these moods, Louise knew it was best to leave him alone.

As he went in the office, he told her he was going to take the Rosenthal case. He didn't notice her frown of displeasure. A few minutes later he asked her to get the district attorney on the line. He wanted to get the boys out of jail and into juvenile hall.

The call lasted quite a while. After he hung up, Louise could hear him pacing up and down in his office. Something hadn't gone right. Soon the intercom signaled her to come in.

"The D. A. won't go for the idea of putting the boys in juvenile hall," Grant announced as soon as she walked in.

This was unusual. Bob Matson had a reputation for trying to help first offenders get straightened out. "But they don't have a record. The charges are serious but not that. . . ."

Grant cut her off. "The charges are armed robbery and first-degree murder." He stopped pacing and looked at her. Her shocked reaction seemed to please him. It continued to please him. He continued pacing. "They insist the boys brought the weapon to the scene."

"But I thought you said. . . ."

"Right," Grant interrupted again. "The boys told me the gun belonged to Rosenthal. This could have a tremendous influence on the judge. A real gun gives the whole case a much different aspect."

Secretly, Louise was half glad. She hoped he would decide not to take it.

"If they've lied to me I'll refuse the case. It's enough to have to worry about the press and what effect it'll have on the people of this city. I'm not going to have to wonder if my clients are telling me the truth."

Louise waited quietly for Grant to settle down.

"Cancel all my morning appointments. I'm going down to the jail first thing tomorrow morning."

Louise sighed, but it was useless to say anything. He wouldn't quiet down until it was settled. And from the way the newspaper was playing up the story and condemning the boys, that was a long way off.

Early the next morning, Grant returned to the jail. A night of rehashing the difference in the two stories hadn't improved his temper. If the boys had lied about this, maybe they lied about other things. A talk with Gary Wilson was first. He seemed to be a leader of sort. This time Grant would make sure he had the truth.

The guard unlocked the door and Grant went in. Gary was lying on the cot reading a paperback book. He got to his feet as soon as he saw Grant.

"Hello, Mr. Williams," he said with genuine gladness. "I wasn't expecting any visitors today."

"I dropped by just for a minute to clarify a point," Grant opened. "How are things?"

"Fine. It gets pretty lonesome, and I bet we're really behind in our school work. Otherwise it's okay."

The simple comment made Grant wonder. Didn't they

understand how serious their crime was? They wouldn't be going back to school as they knew it.

"Let's talk for a while," Grant said, sitting down on the lone chair. "I need to know all of you better to defend you."

Gary dropped down on the cot. He drew his legs up and leaned back against the wall.

"I noticed the book you're reading," Grant said to open the conversation. "Not exactly a classic."

Gary picked up the book and laughed. It wasn't a classic by any stretch of the imagination. "Maybe a bit more realistic than the classics," he answered.

"Do you like classics?"

A frown of concentration crossed his brow. He flipped the pages of the book back and forth as he thought. He did a lot of reading, and this was something he had thought of before. "Classics are all right. I know they represent the finest writing in the world, but the authors are dreamers with hopes of changing the world. That's kind of a lost dream. The world has been going along too long in her set patterns to ever change. Paperback writers seem to feel this. They just write about life as they find it. They think the way I do," he ended.

The answer was more than Grant had expected. "That was almost a discourse. I don't think you came up with that on the spur of the moment."

Gary blushed. "No, Sir. I wrote a theme paper on it."

They talked for a while, comparing types of literature. The boy was well-read. He agreed with Grant that the better literature of the day was taking a disturbingly downward trend, but he wouldn't change his ideas about the paperbacks.

"Where do you get those pulp books?" Grant pointed to the one Gary held.

"Most kids get them down at a drug store. Mark's father owns the company that publishes some of them so Mark usually gets a stack of them for us. We all read them when there's nothing better to do."

The last statement bothered Grant. "Have you ever thought what these books might be doing to your mind?"

Gary looked surprised. "I really hadn't given it much thought."

Grant led the conversation toward the next subject. "What do you think of school generally?"

"It's fine," came a quick reply. "I'm doing all right with my grades. You have to have pretty good grades to play football and be on the track team."

"Are you out for track? That was my sport. They called me 'Toothpick Williams' because my legs were so long and skinny."

A look of real interest came to Gary's face. Grant had found a key. Perhaps it would encourage Gary to talk more freely.

It did. Gary started talking of his plans for college and a career. He had his future laid out step by step. Grant listened and his heart began to ache. Here was a boy with so much to live for and so much to give. Now he was involved in a tragedy that would ruin his whole life. He didn't seem to realize even now that one stupid mistake was going to change all his plans.

"You're outlining quite a future," Grant said when the boy stopped talking. "Your mother must be proud."

"Yeah, I guess so," Gary replied quietly.

"How is she? I haven't had an opportunity to speak with her at any length." He didn't add that he still thought of that first meeting.

"Mom's fine," Gary answered briefly. "She comes every day. She looks her usual calm, efficient self."

His answer was cold and formal. Grant wondered if a problem existed between the two of them.

"Doris told me she had raised you alone. Did you ever know your father?"

"No. I don't remember him. She never talks about him."

The ease and friendliness disappeared. Gary became quiet and reserved. Grant's question had uncovered a prob-

55

lem. What was the extent of it? Was the hostility directed against his father or his mother? Was it strong enough to have motivated the boy's actions? Grant would have to find the answers.

"Well, Gary, it's about time for me to go. I appreciate your talking so freely with me. It's very important that we trust and understand one another."

Gary nodded. He uncrossed his legs and moved to the edge of the cot, ready to get up when Grant did. The mask of unconcern had dropped back between them.

Almost as an after thought in appearance, Grant turned to the reason for his visit. "There's one further question I would like to ask you. I talked to the district attorney yesterday. He said he had evidence to prove you took the murder weapon to the store."

"That's a lie!" Gary shouted angrily. "The only guns we had were the toy guns I bought in the hobby store."

The anger that flashed into the boy's face was the first honest emotion Grant had seen in any of them. "I believe you," he said, realizing that he did believe him. "We'll just have to discover where the gun came from."

The sudden outburst had surprised even Gary. He hadn't thought he cared that much about anything anymore. "Well, I don't much care on my part," he said to cover up his feelings. "I do hate to see the other guys charged with something they didn't do."

"As long as I know the truth, I can help you," Grant promised. He stood up. Gary scrambled to his feet. They shook hands and Grant turned toward the door. He paused a moment before calling the guard.

"Gary, if you could have seen before what this act would cost you, would you still have gone through with it?"

The answer came without hesitation. "I think we all knew we'd get caught, Mr. Williams. It didn't make any difference. We still did it."

"But why, Gary? Why did you do such a foolish thing?"

The young boy bowed his head. "Everyone seems to ask that same question. I don't have the answer. If any of us knew why we were doing it . . . I don't think it would have happened. We just did it."

Grant left the cell relieved and yet depressed. He felt sure the boys had told him the truth. They hadn't taken the gun to the store. He would have to find out where it had come from. That wasn't the main problem. He still was no closer to finding a motive for their action. Without a motive, their case was weak. The papers were already playing up the "thrill murder" and "crime without reason" angle. Why wouldn't they tell him? Didn't they really have any idea?

On the way back to the office, Grant picked up a newspaper. He stared at the headlines, then an angry scowl crossed his face.

LAWYER SEES D.A. WILLIAMS PRESSURES FOR RELEASE OF THREE BOYS

This was the last straw. People accepted too easily anything they read in the paper. With this kind of reporting he'd never be able to get a fair trial for the boys. No judge would grant a juvenile hearing. No jury would give an unbiased decision. It had to stop.

Grant changed his direction and headed for the Daily News. He had never gone to an editor before, but this time circumstances warranted it. In fact, the more he thought about it, the more angry he got.

CHAPTER FIVE

IN THE MAIN OFFICE of the *Daily News*, a half wall with a swinging door separated the editor's secretary from the rest of the office. The door swung open with an angry squeak, then banged back against the post. The secretary looked up into the equally angry eyes of Grant Williams.

"A . . . yes, Sir? Is there something . . .?"

"I want to see the editor," Grant demanded before she could finish her question.

"Oh, I'm sorry, Sir, but Mr. Shadwell can't be disturbed this afternoon. If you'd care to make an appointment. . . ."

Grant could see the editor through the glass partitions that separated his office from the rest of the room. With a look of disgust, he crossed to the door and was in the office before the secretary could protest.

Shadwell looked up from his work when the door opened, an automatic smile on his face. "Good afternoon, Mr. Williams."

"Forget the good part," Grant said, flinging a newspaper across the desk into the editor's lap. He watched with some satisfaction as the smile lessened. "What's this all about?" he demanded.

Shadwell pushed the paper away with an annoyed wave. "I've been half expecting to hear from you. Though I had hoped that you might possibly understand."

"Understand what?"

"Look, Williams, we'll not solve anything yelling at one another. Sit down a minute and let me explain a few things. We're both intelligent men and we're both busy. This won't take long."

"All I want to know is why you're twisting things all around."

The editor flashed a tired smile. "My job is to sell newspapers. I don't manufacture news. I only report what happens in an interesting way for people to read."

"I don't call this reporting. You've so twisted the truth, even God would have a hard time finding it."

"Some people find this hard to believe, Williams, but I am not the watchdog of the public. I'm a businessman like anyone else in this city. I write stories the way people want to read them."

"With no thought of who it might hurt?"

"That's not my responsibility," Shadwell said strongly. "Of course I don't deliberately try to hurt someone, but I do have to sell papers."

"Your responsibility is to help develop the truth, not tear it apart," Grant insisted. "Your influence is too great for you to disregard possible outcomes. You can't condemn anyone before a trial."

Shadwell shook his head slowly. "Come on, Williams, your noble ideas went out with the stone age. Newspapers today are like any other business. We're out to make money. If we don't, we go under. It's as simple as that. Noble ideas don't make money. We take the popular opinion and print it."

It was useless. Grant saw he was getting no help or sympathy from the editor. If he was going to stop the reporting, he would have to go to some other source.

"All right, Mr. Shadwell. I'm sorry I wasted our time. I hope you never find yourself in a similar situation."

He left as swiftly as he had come.

Driving to the office the next morning, Grant reviewed the case in his own mind. So many things were going against him. The district attorney hadn't helped. He didn't know if Matson would even help keep the case in juvenile court. The papers were against him. Even the boys weren't helping him much. For the first time in his career, he felt an inadequacy in the law.

He entered the office building and started toward the elevator, almost colliding with Doris Wilson as she came hurrying out of the coffee shop.

"Why, Mr. Williams, imagine finding you here."

He turned toward her with a questioning look. Surely she couldn't believe him so naive as to think their meeting an accident. Then he met her eyes and saw the teasing innocence. She knew exactly what he was thinking and was laughing at him.

"Good morning, Mrs. Wilson. You're looking lovely today."

"Thank you, Mr. Williams," she answered with his same mock formality. "I came here early this morning in hopes of catching you in the coffee shop before you went upstairs."

"Then I'm sorry I missed you," he said, truly sorry. "What can I do for you?"

"I'd hoped . . . I know you're terribly busy, but I'd hoped you might spare a few minutes of your time for me."

Her self-assurance seemed to slip just a little. Grant felt sorry for her. She needed someone to talk to. In a way he was pleased she had come to him.

"Of course I have time for you. When would you like it to be?"

"Tonight over dinner?"

Grant blinked. "Why, yes . . . that would be fine," he said hastily to cover his surprise.

"I hope you'll forgive my boldness, but it's so much easier to talk in a relaxed atmosphere."

"It's a very good idea. I'm sorry I didn't think of it first," he recovered. "May I pick you up?"

"Why don't we meet somewhere," Doris suggested. "Then it won't take so much of your time. Say the Blue Room at seven."

"I'll be there," Grant promised.

Doris smiled, then turned and left. Grant looked after her until she left the building. She certainly was a fascinating woman. He'd heard so many things about her recently. Were they all true? Maybe he was to find out.

By evening when he met Doris, Grant was still dissatisfied and troubled. Everything was so confused. Nothing was going right. He arrived at the restaurant a few minutes late and found Doris waiting. In tight-lipped silence, he followed the waiter across the room to the table where she sat. He was sure every eye in the room turned as he passed. They all knew who he was and probably considered him the bad guy.

"Good evening," he said crisply when he reached the table.

"Hello," Doris answered gayly. Her greeting was followed by a chuckle.

"What's the matter?" Grant asked in annoyance.

She smiled shyly, quickly appraising his mood. "Forgive me, I didn't mean to laugh." She reached out and brushed his hand lightly. "You must have a lot on your mind. It's just that crossing the room you very much resembled a prisoner following a priest to the death house."

His first reaction was further annoyance. She should be more appreciative of his feelings. This was a time to be serious. He was about to express his feelings, when once again he felt the soft touch of her hand and saw the twinkle in her eyes. His anger softened.

"I must have looked pretty funny at that."

Doris laughed, pleased with her lead. She had succeeded in relaxing him. Now she could lead the conversation in the direction she desired.

"I read the *Daily News*. I would venture to guess it probably had something to do with your mood."

With an angry jerk, Grant pulled his chair closer to the table. "Shadwell is turning the whole city against the boys. He won't listen to reason. I can't understand his irresponsibility. His whole existence can be summed up in one word: money."

"Just don't underestimate him," Doris warned. "He can be a resourceful man if he dislikes you."

That warning was too late. "He's proven that point to me. He's got me labeled as a jerk. Now I know what it feels like to be the bad guy. You shouldn't be seen with me. People will say that I'm forcing my attention on you."

"I wouldn't mind that in the least," Doris said quickly. "They'd be jealous."

Her answer was so quick and so forward, Grant looked at her for a long time. When he realized what she meant, he could find no ready answer and was embarrassed.

Silence fell between them. Doris watched Grant drum his fingers against the table. This wasn't what she had planned when she asked him to dinner. Maybe it was time to leave the dim lights and soft music and all the people he thought were watching him.

"Grant, I'm not at all hungry and I don't think you are either. Why don't we leave here and go for a ride where we can talk. We can stop at some hamburger stand when we're hungry."

"That's an idea," he answered with a chuckle. He could envision them standing up and just walking out. When Doris did stand up, he stared at her dumbfounded. "We can't leave," he protested.

"Watch," she answered with a teasing grin.

She left the table and started for the door. She was gone before he could protest further. If he went after her, he knew what people would think. If he didn't follow her they'd probably think it anyway. Suddenly he didn't care. No matter what he did it was wrong, so he might as well do as he pleased. He got up and followed her out.

Grant drove out into the country. The ride proved to be peaceful and relaxing. Doris displayed a warm and friendly personality. Grant wondered why he had been wary of her. She needed to talk and laugh as much as he did. There really wasn't any reason why they couldn't be friends. They had many things in common. Perhaps all the little things he had heard about her were exaggerations. She had led a hard, lonely life.

The evening passed. With great reluctance, Grant at last turned his car toward home. Very little urging would have kept him out most of the night. Doris knew how discouraged he was feeling. He would probably do whatever she suggested, but she wasn't sure yet. Tonight wasn't the time to ask. Besides, her own feelings were clouding. She was beginning to like him more than she should. This wasn't in accord with her plans.

They reached the apartment house where Doris lived. The arrival had a sobering effect on Grant. As he came around the car to help her out, he wondered what would happen next. Had she misinterpreted his attention? Would she try to invite him up? He couldn't dare accept. No matter how innocent it was, someone would see them and talk.

At the door of the apartment house, Doris turned and held out her hand. "It's been such a delightful evening, Grant. Thank you for being so kind and considerate and such a good listener. I needed someone to talk to."

"The evening has been equally nice for me," Grant replied truthfully. "Sometimes even lawyers need someone to talk to."

"Good. Then maybe we can do it again. Good night, Grant."

She went into the apartment house and the door shut behind her. Grant stood a long moment staring at the door. A deep longing built up within him. He felt lost and alone. The enjoyment of the evening slipped away.

Slowly he walked back to the car and got in. The fragrance of her perfume lingered in the air. He reached down to start the car, then stopped. Where was he going to go? There was no place. He was all alone. Something was wrong. His life seemed empty and meaningless. So many things he'd valued and used as guides now seemed to be disappearing. He had no place to tie his life. There was no place to go and no one to turn to. No one cared.

Grant shook his head hard to rid himself of such feelings. What was the matter with him? Why all of a sudden did he feel so restless? He had been a bachelor a long time. He'd never considered himself a lonely man. He had many friends and outside interests. Why the sudden void?

Had Doris awakened him to this void? Was she showing him something he was missing? Then why did he have that feeling of apprehension about her? He feared to be with her and felt empty and restless when away. Somehow he had to get his life back on an even keel.

With Shadwell's refusal of aid, Grant decided to call the D. A. again and ask his help. He had to get the case transferred to the juvenile authorities. At least judges were more open-minded, and would listen to both sides. A jury couldn't help but be biased by the paper.

When Bob Matson came to the phone, his voice sounded guarded. Grant overlooked it and started right into his arguments.

"Bob, I need your help. I want the case transferred to juvenile court."

Bob was silent a moment. "I don't think I can help you, Grant. I won't say definitely but the way things are going, I'm going to have to ask for an adult trial. The public won't stand for anything else."

"You are all being influenced by the papers, Bob. The boys aren't that bad. They deserve a chance."

"You keep saying that, Grant, and I'd like to believe you, but things keep turning up."

"It looks bad, but the kids aren't that bad. There has to be a reason for what they did. It's just a matter of time before I uncover it."

"It's going to be hard to come up with a convincing reason, Grant. How are you going to explain Mark Hayden

64

as being the one who planned the entire crime? What possible reason could he have?"

Not again, Grant groaned to himself. Were they never going to tell him the truth? How many times was it going to happen? Rich man's son plans crime. How was he going to fight that. "Where did you find this out?" he asked Bob.

"One of the boys let it slip. I'd hoped it was something you weren't aware of. I'd hate to think you were defending clients you knew were wrong. In fact, the way things are going, I hate to see you mixed up in it at all."

"I . . . I don't think the boys are getting a fair shake. They're not that wrong."

"Be sure they're not duping you," Bob warned. "And about the other . . . I won't say no. But I don't think I can help you."

"Okay, Bob. Thanks," Grant said wearily.

Grant hung up. Now he was really in trouble. The way things were going, the boys wouldn't have a chance against a jury. But from what he had learned, did they deserve a chance or were they, as Bob suggested, playing him for a chump. He was going to find out. He was tired of being the last one to find out things about his clients. It was time to have a talk with Mark.

Mark grinned and jumped to his feet as his visitor entered. "Hi, Mr. Williams, how are you?"

"Hello, Mark. How's everything going?" Grant set his briefcase on the floor and sat down on the chair.

"Fine, Sir," Mark replied. He dropped back on the cot. "What do you have today?"

"Questions," Grant replied. "A few more questions."

Mark nodded, then leaned back against the wall.

"Mark, there is one item that I'd like very much to get cleared up. I won't say any of you deliberately lied. . . . but I do think you were leading me to believe something not entirely true."

As he spoke, Grant watched the boy. Mark couldn't

meet his eyes. "I guess it's about the planning," he volunteered.

That was it! Grant was relieved. If Mark knew exactly what the problem was, maybe there wouldn't be any more surprises.

Mark twisted around on the cot to hide his embarrassment. "The fellas . . . well, all of us . . . we decided we wanted to share the blame equally. If it came out that it was my idea . . . with my father's money and all . . . well it would look worse. You know, like we did it for kicks."

"Did you do it for kicks?"

"No, Sir."

"Why did you do it?"

"I . . . I'm sorry, Sir. . . . I don't know."

Grant sighed. Where was he going to find the motive? How far back did he have to go? "Tell me how you went about planning it. Where did you get the first idea?"

The plan had come from a very common source. Mark's father owned a drive-in movie. Mark had a pass to get in. When he had nothing better to do, he went to see a movie. One night he had seen a movie about a robbery. That had started him thinking about the perfect crime. He told his friends about it. They talked at first in fun about committing such a crime. Then, before they realized what was happening, they were planning one of their own. It became a challenge. It was something to work at and beat, but it had all been in fun. Then one day it had happened. No one knew why or how.

It had happened. That was the only explanation Grant seemed to get. It had happened, but now a man was dead and three lives were ruined. There had to be more of a reason.

"Had you ever thought of doing something like this before?" Grant asked.

Mark shook his head. "If I hadn't seen that movie, we probably wouldn't have even talked about it. Lots of kids I know have gotten in trouble over doing things they saw in movies or read about."

"You think the fault lies in having these things around?"

Mark shrugged. "I don't know. Maybe so. My dad is probably to blame for some. If it's around, kids will buy it, because there's nothing better to do. If they couldn't buy it, then they'd find something else to do."

If only he could make the publisher see that, Grant thought. Maybe if Felix Hayden saw what had happened to his son, then maybe he would listen. No, Grant decided, it was a fruitless battle.

"Mark, I have one more question. You're smart boys. You knew what this kind of junk was doing to your minds. Why didn't you leave it alone?"

Sadly he shook his head. "From here looking back, it's easy to see, Mr. Williams. Getting here was another story. One step just led to another. Most of it was something to do. It was available. There wasn't anything else to do. We went farther than we intended to, and now it's too late."

CHAPTER SIX

AFTER TALKING TO MARK, Grant went home instead of back to his office. He felt defeated. The case was going badly. For once he felt very unsure of the law. He knew the boys deserved help, but how was he going to convince anyone.

At home he dropped his briefcase in a chair and went into the kitchen. Cooking was a hobby with Grant. It took his mind off his work.

Paging through the recipe book, he remembered he hadn't called his office. Louise didn't know he wasn't coming back. By now she would have left, but she always gave his messages to the answering service.

He dialed the number, then waited for the gruff voice of the operator. When Louise answered, it surprised him. "Louise, is that you?"

She laughed. "Yes, it is. I've taken a part-time job with the answering service."

"Either that or you're taking up light housekeeping in my outer office. Remember, no cooking privileges."

Again she laughed gayly. "Rest assured, I would never dream of causing such a scandal. I'm just catching up on a few things."

Grant felt guilty. She was working late to catch up on the things he really should be doing. "Don't go putting in a lot of extra hours. Things will slow down when the trial is over. Then we can catch up."

"I'm not really doing that much. Besides, I'm buttering you up for a raise," she said to cover the embarrassment his praise caused her.

"Oh oh, now I'm in trouble. If this keeps up, I'll have to marry you to afford you."

Even in jest, the words struck deep at her heart. She tried to laugh to cover her feelings, but it caught in her throat. Grant heard the little choking sound.

"I called to get any messages," he said.

"Let me see what I have." She shuffled through some papers, using the time to control her voice. "Nothing important," she answered. "Mr. Knight wants to change his will again. That's it."

"Good," Grant said. "I didn't want to work tonight. Thanks, Louise, and now get home."

He was just about to hang up, when her voice stopped him. "Wait! I almost forgot. Mrs. Wilson called and asked that you call her back."

"Doris? What did she want?" The moment the first name slipped out, Grant regretted it. First names gave the relationship a more personal sound than he wanted anyone to think.

"She wouldn't say," Louise replied evenly. "She asked that you return the call."

"All right, Louise. Thank you."

He hung up. Then he leaned back in his chair and groaned. He had done it again. Louise was certain to think the worst. He hadn't even thought to ask for the telephone number. Try as he might, he couldn't seem to keep himself from an involvement. The whole city was probably convinced that he was having an affair. Let them, he decided. He didn't care any more. But he did care — especially with Louise.

He picked up the telephone again to call Doris. Halfway through the numbers, he stopped. Was this what he wanted to do? He was sure Doris wanted only to talk. It seemed that she was calling more frequently lately. Perhaps Louise did have grounds for her suspicions.

Tonight he was going to forget everything connected

with the trial and spend an evening at home with his books. He didn't want to think about the case, women, the office or anything else.

He finished his dinner, did up the few dishes, then went into the den to read. The front page of the paper was filled with pictures and stories of the case. After a few minutes, he threw it down in disgust. He picked up the book he was reading, then dropped it. He wasn't in a mood for serious reading.

Finally he got up and wandered through the house. Tonight it seemed terribly quiet. He was restless. He wanted to do something, but what? He wandered back to the telephone. Maybe he should call Doris. She might really have a problem. It wasn't fair for him to make her wait all this time.

He dialed the number. The telephone rang five times before Doris answered. His ego deflated. He had been so sure she was standing by the phone waiting for his call. The casualness of her greeting further deflated him.

"I'm sorry I'm so late in calling," he said, embarrassed by his silly ideas. "I was away from the office all day."

"That's all right, Grant. I wasn't sure the message had been relayed to you."

He understood her meaning. "Louise is careful with all my calls," he said.

This seemed to satisfy her. Her voice warmed up. "I called earlier to invite you here for dinner. The thought of being alone was depressing. But it's late . . ."

She trailed her sentence, leaving the suggestion open to him. He suddenly realized that he didn't want to be alone this night either.

"Maybe it's not too late. I've eaten, but we can still go for a ride."

"I'd like that very much."

"Good. I'll be there in fifteen minutes."

Doris remained seated by the telephone after Grant

hung up. Her plan was advancing. She should feel exhilarated. This was what she wanted. But was it, really?"

When she had first gone to Grant Williams, she had been single-minded in purpose. She wanted Gary out of jail. Everyone she talked with felt Williams was the best one for the job. She had used all the means at her disposal to get him to take the case. Now she wanted to go one step further. She wanted to insure his winning Gary's freedom. She had a plan, and Grant was the intricate part of it. Her plan was going well. If only Grant weren't so nice. Maybe if she had met a man like him before, she might have been able to straighten out her life. Now . . . it was too late.

She hadn't always been this way — selfishly using other people to obtain her desires. Where had she changed? Had she married too young? Perhaps if she had been more forgiving of Gary's father. A man can make a mistake. When it had happened, her only thoughts were of revenge. She wanted to hurt him. Gary was her means. She had taken the boy away and had never let him see his father. She had even planted a grain of hate for his father in the boy's mind.

From that time on, Doris had hated all men, and had used them only to fit her purposes. She couldn't have cared less what happened to them. Then she met Grant.

Each time she went with Grant, Doris found it harder to keep her mind on her plan. He was so kind and understanding — so handsome and intelligent — so little boyish in some of his ideas. Doris stopped in her thinking. Was she falling in love with Grant? The idea felt good. No! She stopped herself. This couldn't be. Gary had to come first. Oh, Grant, why did you have to come along too late?

Grant arrived at the apartment house right on time. They decided to ride out into the country, remembering how much fun they had had the first time. Grant helped her on with her coat, took her arm as they went out, and helped her into the car. Doris noticed all these little courtesies. It increased her problem. Could she sacrifice him to enact her plan? She had to.

Once they left the lights of the city behind, the night became clear and quiet. For a while they talked of little things, letting their cares fly with the wind rushing past the window. For a while they rode in silence. The worries that had seemed so pressing in the city now fled.

Time rushed by, spent all too swiftly by the enjoyment. Soon it was late, and Grant had to turn the car toward the city. As they drove back Doris, unlike Grant, seemed to pick up the troubles she had dropped on the way. Her problem returned. She had to complete her plan.

At the apartment house, Grant turned the car to the curb and stopped. He had felt her tension mount and wondered what was wrong. As he turned, he saw the street light reflected in the tears flowing down her cheeks.

"Doris, what is it?"

His voice was so soft and gentle, so filled with concern. She knew she couldn't answer without crying. She needed him, but was afraid of her need.

"Nothing is the matter," she said forcefully. "It's been a lovely evening and I enjoyed every minute. Thank you for the ride." Her words came faster, nearing hysterics.

Grant reached out to touch her shoulder. He wanted to comfort her — to show her that he understood — to let her know she wasn't alone. Suddenly he found her in his arms. Almost without thinking, he bent down and kissed her.

All the magic of the evening, and the longing and loneliness they both felt flowed into the kiss. Doris wanted so much to let the love develop, but she knew it would keep her from her purpose.

She pulled away. They looked at one another for a long moment, wondering at the swiftness of the events. He started to lean toward her again, but she held him away.

"No, Grant."

Her words were spoken softly, but they broke the spell.

Grant leaned back. What had happened to him? He started to apologize, but Doris placed her finger across his lips.

"Don't," she whispered. "Don't say anything. It was too nice . . . just this way."

She opened the car door and was gone. What did she mean? What did she want? Had she shared his sudden feelings? Was he in love? It wasn't what he expected, and it made him feel carefree and wild.

As Grant was leaving for the office the next morning, the telephone rang. Could it be Doris, he wondered. Overnight his feelings had cooled, leaving him with an unanswered question. What was their new relationship to be?

He picked up the receiver. Instead of Doris, Judd was on the line. Grant was both relieved and disappointed. Judd asked to see him before work, and Grant agreed.

When Grant drove up, Judd was waiting in front of the building. Grant parked and joined him.

"Let's get a cup of coffee down the street," Grant suggested. "It's not as crowded as the coffee shop here."

They walked a short way in silence before Judd spoke out. "I've been giving a lot of thought to the murder case and the boys and I think maybe I can help you."

"How's that?" Grant asked.

"If I went to the jail and talked with the boys, I might be able to understand them and find out why they acted as they did. I've worked with boys enough to know how to reach them."

"I wish someone could reach them," Grant admitted. "I don't seem to be getting very far myself. I'm no closer to a motive now than when I started."

"You might even be able to use me as some kind of an authority to testify for them," Judd volunteered further.

This was a step farther, Grant thought. It might work. With Judd's background, he could be called an authority on the subject. If he found the boys to be good, maybe the judge would listen.

They reached the restaurant and the conversation switched abruptly. At the door they found something else to occupy their minds.

"Look who's waiting for us."

Across the room sat a reporter from the *Daily News*. He was watching the two men with sharp interest.

"It's not going to do you any good to be seen with me," Grant warned.

Judd shook his head. "He doesn't worry me. I agree with what you're doing and I don't care who knows it."

"I know that, Judd, but I'm worried about Shadwell. I don't know what to expect from him. With you trying to gain support for your youth center, I don't want to upset the cart."

Grant deliberately brought up Judd's plans for a youth center. It was something the minister had been working on for a long time. Some bad publicity from Shadwell could conceivably ruin a few plans.

Without hesitation, Judd replied. "If the Lord wants Grace Brethren to have a swimming pool and a bowling alley for their young people, He'll see that we get it. And when a Christian minister reaches the point that he can't stand up for what he believes in, then he no longer belongs in the ministry."

Shrugging his shoulders, Grant led the way into the restaurant. "I could use some help, but from now on watch yourself," he said.

Jo Ann stood at the corner and stared at the office building across the street. Today was the day. She had to do it today. If only she weren't so frightened. She hadn't been this scared since the night she had met John behind the drugstore. How long ago that now seemed. So much had happened. It almost seemed that she was leading the life of someone else. She kept wondering when she would wake up and find it was all a terrible dream.

The traffic cleared. Gathering up her courage, Jo Ann walked bravely across the street. Inside, she saw the building directory across the lobby by the elevator. Her steps echoed on the marble floor as she crossed the room. She found the name she was seeking:

GRANT WILLIAMS — ATTORNEY-AT-LAW

Each day for the last week she had left school during the lunch hour and had hurried to the drugstore across the street. From the window she had watched until the lawyer left for lunch. It was almost the same time every day.

This morning she had decided it would have to be today. She couldn't sneak away from school every lunch hour without being caught. It was senseless to wait any longer. All she had to do was walk up to him and ask. The worst he could say was no.

The clock over the elevator struck twelve-fifteen. It was late. She wondered if she had missed him. Perhaps he wasn't coming down for lunch today. Jo Ann felt relieved, then disappointed. She had come this far, it was a shame not to go on.

The elevator bell sounded and the doors opened. Grant stepped out alone. He glanced at Jo Ann, smiled absently, then headed for the front doors. At the coin newsrack he stopped to get a copy of the early edition.

Unable to speak out, Jo Ann watched him walk away. She had meant to call to him as soon as he stepped from the elevator, but seeing the famous lawyer so close had frightened her. He went by before she recovered. She was about to leave in defeat when she noticed him stopping to get a newspaper. This time she wasn't going to fail.

Grant folded the paper under his arm and turned toward the front door. He heard the hurried steps crossing the marble floor behind him, and over his shoulder he saw the same young girl approaching. He pulled the door open, and waited for her to precede him out. When she saw him waiting, her steps faltered.

"Can I help you?" he offered. "Are you looking for someone?"

The girl stopped. "Are . . . are you Mr. Williams?"

"Yes, I am." He stepped back to her.

"My name is . . . Barbara," Jo Ann lied. "Barbara Gills. I . . . I have a letter for one of your clients."

Grant frowned. "Who is it you want to reach?" He was suspicious.

"I have a letter for John Fieldings."

Her answer gave Grant the key to her identity. He looked at her closely and the description fit. Combining the hesitation and fright, he knew she could be only one person. "Are you Jo Ann?" he asked gently.

The question startled her. She hadn't expected him to have ever heard of her. Without thinking she nodded.

Grant looked around the lobby. They couldn't stand in the middle of the floor to talk. Next to the telephone was an alcove. Taking Jo Ann by the arm, he led her toward it.

"John has told me a great deal about you," he said as they walked. "He says you're a wonderful girl."

His words brought a light to the young girl's eyes. "How is he?" she asked eagerly.

"He's fine, Jo Ann. He misses you, but he's fine."

She leaped at the words. "Does he miss me? I was afraid that he . . . I haven't heard from him since . . . since that night."

"He hasn't tried to get in touch with you because he knows how your parents feel," Grant explained.

Jo Ann frowned. "My parents and I don't see things in the same light. Now that John's in trouble and needs help, they want me to forget him."

The problem was plain. Jo Ann felt that she was in love with John and wanted to stick by him. Her parents were trying to get her to forget him, and Grant couldn't blame them for their efforts. What parent couldn't see that there was little chance of a happy ending!

"I'm sure your parents are only doing what they feel is best for you, Jo Ann. Your future happiness is their main concern."

Jo Ann sighed. "Oh, I suppose I know that. If I were in their shoes, I might even feel the same. I just wish they wouldn't be so closed-minded. They insist John is wrong, and I should forget him."

"And what do you think, Jo Ann? Do you really think John was right? Or are you protecting him to rebel against your parents?"

Anger appeared in her face. She started to hotly deny his accusation, then stopped. This man was trying to help her.

"I have wondered about my feelings," she admitted. "I can't understand why John did such a thing, but I guess we all do things and don't know why. Maybe what he did was wrong, but he's not bad, and I still love him."

"I'm not encouraging you to go against your parents, Jo Ann. You must obey them. I can tell you that John feels the same way. When the time comes for him to start over, he's going to need a lot of help. Maybe you'll be the one to give it to him."

Jo Ann smiled, and for that moment she was a grown woman. "If I can do that, I will be completely happy."

Grant glanced at his watch. He was far behind schedule. "Jo Ann, I'm afraid I'm going to have to go. I have a luncheon engagement that I'm already late for. I'll tell John that I saw you."

"Ah . . . Mr. Williams . . ."

He waited.

"I still have this letter for John. I don't know how to send it. Would you . . .?" Her voice stopped but her eyes pleaded with him.

"I'll make a deal," he said. "I'll give the letter to John this time if you'll promise not to go against your parents' wishes again."

"I promise," she answered quickly. "I didn't like doing it this time."

"Now it's time for us both to scoot."

With a quick step, Jo Ann stood up on her toes and placed a kiss on the lawyer's cheek. "You're wonderful."

She turned and ran from the building. Grant looked after her, touching his cheek where she had kissed him. He smiled, but it was a sad smile. They were two nice kids, and so young to bear such a burden. In a couple of years they would have married and settled down to a normal life. Now, a few minutes of folly had changed their whole future.

It was so senseless, so needless. How could they have done it? Grant wanted to help them, but he couldn't even seem to understand how they thought or what motivated them. Was every generation so separated from their offspring? Had his own father had the same difficulty in understanding him? Grant thought not, but this generation was different. It was a rebel. But why? Had a part of the system broken down? Or was it slowly crumbling and falling in ruin?

The next day Grant delivered the letter. John was the quiet one of the three for Grant hadn't been able to get him to talk much. He hoped the letter would help.

When he reached the cell, John was on his bunk staring up at the ceiling.

"Hello, John. How are you?"

The boy scrambled to his feet. "Fine, Sir. I wasn't expecting anyone."

Grant sat on the only chair in the cell, and pulled out a pack of gum. He offered a stick to John, then unwrapped a piece for himself. "Don't you have visitors in the afternoon?"

"Not usually. My folks both work during the day. One of them tries to get here every night."

"It must get lonely," Grant sympathized.

John nodded, but didn't answer.

"I saw Jo Ann yesterday."

The name lit up John's eyes. It had been so long since he had seen her. He thought of her every day; tormenting himself for what he had almost done to her and to them. She was the only thing in the world that mattered to him.

How close he had come to ruining her life. Did she still care?

Then fear entered his mind. Why had Mr. Williams gone to see her? Surely he wasn't going to involve her. "You're not getting her into this mess are you?"

"No, John. That wouldn't accomplish anything. She came to see me." Grant pulled the letter from his pocket. "She asked me to give this to you."

John's hand trembled as he took the letter. Tenderly he held it, turning it over and over. What would it say? Did he dare hope? It had been so long. If only he were alone to read it now.

Grant read the longing in the boy's eyes. He stood up. "I'll leave you for a few minutes."

"Oh, no, Sir," John protested guiltily. "I can wait until later. Your time is too important."

He gave the boy a pat on the shoulder. "I can spare a few minutes."

"Thank you," John said, trying to hide his eagerness.

Grant left the room and followed the officer to his desk. "I wanted to give him time to read a letter," he explained.

"That's all right," the officer replied. "You can sit in here with me. Want a cup of coffee?"

"Sounds good."

The officer filled two cups from a pot behind the desk, then handed one to Grant. They silently drank their coffee for several minutes. Then the officer spoke.

"You know, those boys really have us puzzled."

"How's that?"

"Well, I've been here for a good many years. Quite a number of boys have passed through here, and the number seems to go up every year. Most of them are mean and hard — you have to watch them every minute. Your boys . . . they're different. They're quiet and polite and agreeable. You couldn't ask for nicer young fellas."

"They are good boys."

"That's what puzzles us. How did they get into trouble?"

The same question — it's always the same question. Why did such nice kids kill a man? Grant swirled the coffee around in his cup as he thought. What was the reason? What terrible thing had so controlled their minds to allow them to act so? There had to be an answer.

"It's a hard question," Grant finally replied. "I still don't have the complete answer."

"Most people have the wrong idea about those boys. My wife was one of them. She had been reading the paper, and you should have heard what she thought about them. She said they were all cold-blooded killers and deserved at least life in prison. I told her what they were really like, and you know what she said?"

Grant shook his head.

"She said I could convince her, but I'd never be able to convince the rest of the city. As far as they were concerned, the boys were cold-blooded killers, and they didn't care what happened to them."

His words didn't surprise Grant. Most people accepted what they read in the papers without thinking.

"I have two boys almost their age," the officer continued. "We've tried our best to raise them. I can't help but wonder if something like this could happen to them."

Neither man attempted an answer.

The letter was out of sight when Grant returned to the room, but it's influence remained. John seemed happier than Grant had ever seen him.

"From the look on your face, I would say the news in the letter was all good."

John grinned sheepishly. "It was."

"Good."

The atmosphere had changed. Grant sat down in the same chair. Now maybe John would talk a little more. "It must be lonesome in here," he began. "You say your parents come often."

"They come. We probably see more of each other now than we did before, but it hasn't made any difference. We're still like strangers, not knowing what to say to one another." John tried to keep his voice light, but a hurt was there.

"It's hard on them, too," Grant suggested. John nodded, but didn't speak. The shell was returning. Grant quickly changed the subject. "Jo Ann is a fine girl."

Again her name brought a quick smile. "She is. I'm pretty fortunate. I just hope it works out all right."

"That's a lot to hope for when so much has happened."

The boy nodded. "I want to be sure she isn't involved in any way."

"She won't be, John, if she wasn't a part of it."

"She wasn't. If she had been involved, it never would have happened. If she had been home that night . . . if only I could have seen her . . ."

John had to blink hard to keep the tears from showing. It hurt to even think about it. All their plans . . . all the wonderful things they were going to do . . . he had ruined everything. In spite of it all, she still loved him.

"What night did you mean, John?"

"The night we planned the robbery — that God-forsaken night. If only I'd had someone to talk to." He leaned forward, resting his arms on his knees.

"Tell me about it. What happened?"

John remained silent. He wanted to talk, but he didn't know how to begin. He twisted his ring around and around on his finger. "I listened," he finally said.

"Listened to what, John? What was strong enough to make you forget Jo Ann?"

John tried to answer, but he couldn't find the words. He shrugged and bowed his head. "I don't know."

"What happened? I need to know to be able to help."

"I don't know what happened. I didn't plan to get involved, but things started happening. A guy . . . can't fight alone forever."

His words were choked with hidden tears. Grant

wanted to comfort him, but first he had to find out all that had happened.

"One night we were all together having a bull session," John began. "One of the guys starting talking about this movie he had seen. It was supposed to be the perfect crime, but the guy got caught. We started talking about what we'd do to improve it. Just for the fun of it, we started planning a robbery. We really didn't mean it — we were just talking. When I realized what was happening, I felt sick, but by then it was too late. It was senseless . . . but it happened.

"That night, after I had listened to all the plans, I had a feeling we had gone too far; that maybe it might happen. I needed someone to talk to — someone to tell me how to stop the foolishness before it got out of hand. First I went to Jo Ann's. I knew if I could tell her, she'd help me and tell me what to do to stop it — but no one was home."

He stopped speaking. Grant waited, feeling there was more to the story — the most important part. "Then what happened, John? You knew it was wrong, why did you do it?"

John refused to look up or to speak. He had remembered all he wanted to, but Grant needed more.

"Were your parents home? Did you try to talk to them?"

Suddenly John laughed. It was a cruel, bitter laugh, so unlike the quiet, serious boy. What had happened that night? Grant had to know.

"Wouldn't your parents help you?"

"Oh, they would have," John said sarcastically. "They'd have done everything possible to stop it from happening — if they had known. The only thing was . . . they couldn't take time to find out."

Once again he stopped. He hid his face, but Grant saw the sobs shaking his shoulders. "John, tell me about that night," he urged gently. The boy shook his head. "John, I must know — to help the others."

82

For a while John thought. Then he shrugged and straightened up. "Okay, if it'll help the others. It's too late for me now.

"Both my folks work. Sometimes it isn't so bad, but other times I hate it. It was always the other guy's mom who drove us to ball games, or helped with class parties. My mom was always excused because she worked.

"The worst part was that even when they were home they didn't have time. They were always in a hurry. There was never enough time to do all the things they wanted to do. When time ran out, it was my ball game or my trip to the park that was left out."

John sought to keep a casualness in his voice, but the hurt he felt was too great. The tragic part was that his story was the story of thousands of kids. They were given every toy money could buy, and all they really wanted was for dad to play ball or mom to rock them to sleep.

The Fieldings' home had at first seemed ideal to Grant. It looked as though these parents truly loved and were concerned about their son, but now he saw they really didn't have time for him.

"The only thing I ever asked for that my parents never gave me, was more of their time. They meant to, but it never worked out. That night after leaving Jo Ann's, more than anything else I wanted to talk to them. They would have known what to do. If they had only listened . . . ."

His voice trailed off into a husky whisper. The tragedy could so easily have been diverted. He wanted to cry — cry for what he had lost. He stopped and took a deep breath. As the breath escaped, he closed the wall around him and locked himself back inside an attitude of unconcern. The rest of the story he recited.

"There were several cars parked out front when I got home. It was bridge night. I knew I should go to my room and wait until everyone left, but I couldn't. I had to talk to someone right away. I felt it was more important than anything else.

"I went in the back door. Mom was fixing refreshments in the kitchen. She started to listen to me then remembered something she had forgotten to fix. Then, too, someone yelled for her to come bid, and she ran out telling me to wait a minute.

"Finally she sent my dad in. He was in a hurry to get back, but I couldn't get the story out that fast. He wanted to help me but it wouldn't come out fast enough. I gave up, and he went back mad. After that I couldn't talk to anyone. It didn't seem to matter what happened, so I decided to go along with the fellas."

The story ended. It had all happened so simply. With almost no effort a life was ruined and yet so little time would have been needed to avoid the tragedy. How broken-hearted his parents would be when they found out. They worked hard to give him everything, only to miss the one thing he really needed — a little of their time.

On the trip back to the office, Grant stopped to get a copy of the afternoon edition of the *Daily News*. He had learned to expect the worst. Time and again Shadwell was finding ways to keep interest in the case alive. Grant picked up a copy and stood on the corner to read the headlines:

MINISTER REFUSES TO CONDEMN THREE BOYS FOR CRIME

There was a picture of Judd on the front page. The story beneath was not complimentary, and Grant felt guilty for letting his friend get involved. Lawyers were paid to endure such criticism, but ministers were hurt by it. How would the city accept this? Judd was a leading figure. Surely no one would believe what it said, but he knew they would.

By the time he returned to his office, Grant was convinced that the whole world had changed. All his old values were gone. He stepped inside his office. There to greet him was Louise, smiling and unchanged, and a feeling of relief passed over him.

"Louise! You don't know what a relief it is to see you sitting there."

A bemused smile crossed her lips. "Is that a compliment or a warning I'm soon to be turned out to pasture?"

"Today it's the nicest compliment I could pay anyone," he said with a low bow. "To see you sitting there, the way you have for ten years, has made my day complete."

Louise shook her head and sank back in her chair. "Maybe it helped your day, but it has certainly ruined mine. It was unfair to remind me how long I've been here. I'm in a terrible rut."

"No, you're not." Grant cried out in mock horror. "You've become a first-class legal secretary." He threw up his hands in dismay. "But, you'll probably up and marry any day now."

For the second time in a few days, marriage had popped into their conversation. It brought a flush to her cheek. "I don't think I'll be doing that."

An awkward silence fell between them, and Grant looked at her. What had come between them? They almost felt ill at ease.

"I thought we might lock the front office and then concentrate on cleaning up some of the backlog," he suggested uncertainly. "Then we can work without interruption. That is, if you don't mind working a little late?"

"I don't mind at all," she replied quickly, refusing to meet his eyes. "Should I switch the telephone to the answering service?"

Grant snapped his fingers. "Good idea. I never would have thought of it."

He left Louise and stepped into his office. It was dark, cool and quiet inside — a haven from the outside madness. In the room he could begin to pick up the familiar patterns of his life.

The office and the law it represented had been the center of his life for some years. Now it was being pulled away. No, he wasn't going to let it. The law was right, and it was going to win out. He would have to work harder. He wasn't going to let this case defeat him.

Louise entered, her arms full of folders. "I took the liberty of ordering a sandwich and coffee. You look famished," she explained when their eyes met.

"Thank you. It's what I need."

She set the folders on the desk before him, then scurried from the room. "Back in a minute."

Leaning forward in his chair, he took the top folder from the stack and started to read it. His mind didn't want to focus on the material his eyes were covering. His thoughts danced around. He found himself thinking of Louise and what a comfort it had been to find her sitting there. She seemed to know his needs before he was even aware of them. He hadn't even realized he was hungry until she mentioned food. She knew him so well. Was it because they had worked together so long or did she have some special feelings? Could it be, after all these years, that Louise was in love with him? There he went again. Where was he getting these wild ideas?

He dropped the folder to the desk and leaned back in his chair. His brow wrinkled in concentration. The thought was intriguing — he liked Louise. She had a nice personality, a pleasant appearance. They got along well. Perhaps, after all these years, a closer relationship might be permissible.

Grant stopped himself. What was he doing? His life was becoming complicated enough with one woman. What could he ever do with two?

The door opened and Louise came in with a tray from the restaurant. The food looked good, and she set it in front of him. "There now," she said stoutly, trying to overcome the blush. "You're going to eat while I tell you what's been happening in your office."

He grinned boyishly. She smiled back, thinking how terribly handsome he was when he grinned.

"Fair enough," he agreed. "But first of all there are two very important questions I want to ask you."

She sat down next to the desk and nodded for him to proceed.

86

"You've been working with me on the Rosenthal case and you know how much it disturbs me. I've felt that the motive is the key to the case. If it is strong enough and unusual enough, we could convince the judge he should be lenient. So far I haven't been able to find a motive. Now I'm wondering if I'm overlooking it in some way. What do you think?"

Louise paused before answering. It was a habit she had picked up from him. "When you accepted the case, I had a feeling it would be difficult, and I think you've stated the reason why. I don't think you're going to find a single motive that will explain the whole crime. It's going to be a combination of many reasons that happened to come together at the wrong time."

From anyone else, Grant would have dismissed the idea immediately. He was building a defense around finding this motive. The idea that one didn't exist was too frightening to consider. There had to be a reason to make three outstanding young men commit such a deed. There had to be a strong motive, not a combination of little ones.

Louise stirred slightly, bringing him out of his thoughts. She had answered his first question and now was waiting for the second one. After the seriousness of the first, Grant was embarrassed to ask the second. He tried to think of a substitute, but he couldn't.

"Second question. After ten years of working together, I feel we know one another sufficiently well for me to ask you to dinner. Would you consider dining out with a grumpy old lawyer?"

He wanted to sound carefree and casual, but Louise took it differently. She lowered her eyes. When she answered, her voice was barely more than a whisper.

"Why, yes, Grant, I would like that."

Grant groaned inwardly. If she had been casual, it would have been all right. But she was trying hard to be correct and hide her feelings — this gave her away.

"End of questioning," he said. "Now to work."

CHAPTER SEVEN

THAT EVENING GRANT picked up an old classic and settled into his well-worn chair in the den to read. He opened the book to the page he had marked days before. Lately he hadn't been reading much.

For a few pages he read faithfully, then his mind began to wander. The ideas Louise had suggested that afternoon continued to trouble him. If she was right, and no motive developed, he was in trouble. He had built his entire case around the discovery of a motive strong enough and unusual enough to have caused the deed, but a motive that would never be repeated. If he proved this, the judge might put the case in juvenile court and the boys would have a chance to pick up their lives again.

The telephone rang. The unexpected sound made Grant jump. Now what? he thought. What he didn't need was more problems. He debated whether or not he should answer when it rang again. Wearily, he got to his feet and walked into the living room.

It was Judd. The minister apologized for calling so late, but asked if he might come over for a while. Grant immediately thought of the article in the paper. He had meant to call Judd about it, but so many things had happened, he hadn't had a chance.

"I'm not doing a thing, Judd, come on over. I feel like a good discussion."

Judd laughed, but Grant could hear the tension in his voice. "I'll be there in a few minutes," Judd replied.

While he waited, Grant made a pot of coffee and had it ready in the den when Judd arrived. "You look comfortable tonight," Judd said, following him into the den. "Of course, in a room like this, anyone could be comfortable. Why don't you donate it to the church?"

The lawyer laughed. "Come on, Judd. I happen to know you have a study in the rectory."

"True," Judd admitted ruefully. "Somehow though . . . with Diane's playpen in the middle of it, it doesn't have quite the same atmosphere."

"Well, it goes to prove that a man can't have a wife, a daughter and a study, too. Which one will you give up?"

Judd considered the question. "Right now, with Diane cutting teeth, I might consider trading her off. Maybe she'll even call you grandpa again."

The memory brought a chuckle from both men. "You'll never convince me, Judson Lowell, that your lovely wife didn't put Diane up to that. And please note that I am nowhere near old enough to be Diane's grandfather."

"I promise to inform Carolyn," Judd pledged solemnly. "You know we were talking about you tonight."

"Oh, oh, what have I done now?"

"Carolyn commented on what a fine trustee you'd make. You don't drink or smoke or gamble or run around, and you have the professional background. We both agree you could do a good job."

Judd was smiling as he spoke, but there was a serious overtone in his voice.

"Maybe, Judd, some day. Right now this case is taking all my time."

Reluctantly, Judd followed the change in subject. Some day the right time would come. He had to be patient. Christ had His time. "I've given it a little thought myself," he said. "That article in the paper was a shock."

"It was bad. I should have warned you about that reporter. Did you talk to him after I left?"

Judd nodded. "It wouldn't have made any difference. I thought I could handle him. As it happened, I'm not as smart as I thought. He made my words say different things."

"They're good at that. Have you had any problems?"

"A . . . yes . . . a few phone calls. They weren't exactly congratulating me on my stand."

"Shadwell doesn't seem to care much who he's hurting."

"The current trend is to be hard on kids so they won't repeat their crime. People accept the idea, and they don't like anyone going against it."

"But it's not the answer, Judd. These kids need a firm helping hand. With time and understanding, most of them could straighten up. Jail isn't the answer."

"Time is the answer," the minister agreed, "but people seem to spend everything on kids but time. Now adults realize they don't know kids, and they're afraid of them."

"Afraid of them? What do you mean?"

"Remember your own youth. You had no responsibilities, no ties; you were filled with endless energy and enthusiasm searching for an outlet. Kids are crusaders. They want something to dedicate their lives to. I found this out when I worked with them. They don't know the dearness of life or the closeness of death. They need something to work and fight for. We've failed to give it to them."

Listening to the minister, Grant began to see how far he had withdrawn from the younger generation. Maybe he wasn't the right one for the case, but it was too late now.

"There's more," Judd continued. "We've succeeded by our lustful living in destroying this generation's respect for parents and adults. With all the advancements, they have more power than any kids before them have had. We're turning them toward evil, and soon we won't be able to control them. There's enough potential in them to destroy the nation. People are starting to wake up to the fact, and the only solution they've come up with so far is to throw them all in jail."

"What do we do?"

Judd shook his head. "I don't know — discipline or

understanding. Either one is a makeshift answer, a partial correction for damage past done."

"That could explain the attitude of the city — they're afraid. I can't understand these boys myself and I haven't found a clue to a motive."

"Maybe you're not going to find one as such."

The minister's answer startled Grant. Twice in one day this suggestion had been made. Could Judd and Louise have talked together? He thought not.

"Each boy had problems. The problems aren't so large as to be dangerous by themselves, but they make the kids discontented and restless. Put them all together and the problems could destroy their wills to resist. When an opportunity of crime appears, there is no reason to resist. I've seen it happen before in the slums where I worked. There's only so much a person can take."

Could this be right, Grant wondered? If it was, the potential danger was frightening. "If what you suggest is right, this city and probably the whole country is in serious trouble. The problems these boys faced are as common as yesterday."

Judd listened as Grant ran down the line of things he had found. Mark had been raised with a strict, moral sense. First he discovered that morals were good only for some things, and business wasn't one of them. Then he found that his father used them only when it served his purpose. Gary came from a broken home; he was raised without the strong guidance of a father. John's parents had let their life get too busy for a son. They tried to show their love with objects instead of time. The boys had cluttered their minds with trash called modern literature. These were all simple, everyday problems. Add them to the world problems the kids were facing . . . was this the answer?

"What we've come up with is frightening, Grant," Judd said. "These conditions are found everywhere. It's more serious than I thought."

"I know. Look at the rise in juvenile delinquency and

the areas it's coming from. It's not all slums. More and more middle-class kids are getting in trouble. There's a breakdown in our homes and our communities."

"Then I fear for our country," Judd said.

Grant paused. The idea was growing all out of proportion. Was this a key to the behavior of the young? If such common problems could band together to cause good boys to murder, what did the future hold?

"It's frightening all right," Grant concluded. "If society can corrupt fine boys, what's happening to the others?"

"It tells me one thing," Judd said. "The church has a big responsibility. These kids need someone to give meaning and direction to their lives. Christ is the One who can do it — He has all the answers for the world."

Grant didn't agree. He hesitated, hating to hurt the young minister. But what he was thinking was fact. Maybe too many men hadn't spoken in the past.

"I dislike saying this, Judd, but I'm not convinced that Christianity is the answer and not part of the problem."

Judd frowned, but didn't speak. He was worried. He knew by now that Grant didn't speak out against something unless he had ample reason.

"At one time Christianity was strong in this country and influenced society."

"It still does. There are more churches every year."

"I'll agree to part of that," Grant continued. "Christianity is strong in number, but not in character. At one time your churches were uncompromising. If a man was a Christian, people knew it because he was different."

"Times have changed," Judd argued. "If a man tries to stand out like that today, he'll be labeled a fanatic."

"Does that mean you should take a step downward and conform to the world's standards?"

"No, of course not," Judd had to admit. There were many theories to explain the changes in Christianity, but not one of them was of any help to him now. Grant had seen a failure where he knew one didn't belong.

"If Christianity is what you say it is, Judd, there should

be a difference. Today, society is molding the church. However a man wants to live, he just finds a church that allows his way. Your people do lip service, but their hearts and minds are elsewhere. You know . . . I can't help but feel sorry for your Christ. If He did die for this whole world, how can He help but feel He made a terrible mistake?"

The words Grant spoke were honest, but they hurt the minister. He took all the criticism as personal failures. If only he could find the right answers for Grant, for he wanted to help him see.

"If you could show me where even your church is really doing something, then I might be nearer to accepting your Christ for what you claim."

Judd's answer came slow and deliberate. "I know that what you've said is true, for much is to be desired in our churches. But the church is not the important element in God's plan. Men answer to Him personally. The failure of a church isn't a valid excuse for turning from Him."

The lawyer smiled sadly. "I'm sorry, Judd. I can't see where being a Christian will give me any more than I have right now. If your Christ can't answer the problems of His own people, I don't see how He can answer mine."

"It's our fault," Judd pleaded. "It's man's failure — not Christ's. He has the absolute answer, but too many of us just won't accept them."

Grant shrugged his shoulders. "Really, what difference does it make. If Christ has the answer and men can't find it, then the world is still without the answer. Christianity has failed as much as the rest of society. I still believe the answer lies in my law. In the end, it will prove right."

When Judd left his friend's house, he carried with him the depression Grant had felt. The church was truthfully at fault, and he took the full brunt. The longer he pondered, the greater the load became. After all, wasn't he the pastor of Grace Brethren. Wasn't it the largest, most influential church in the city? What kind of an example had he set?

93

What had he done to lessen the problem? The one possible claim was the proposed youth center. He had planned it to be a place for kids to play and have fun, but even that was hopelessly bogged down in the board of trustees.

The load became almost too heavy to bear. Was he a failure? He couldn't go on alone — he needed help. He had to find a quiet place where he could regain his peace.

A few blocks away, Judd remembered a small prayer chapel with doors that never closed. It was maintained for the destitute and wanderers, and tonight that fit him.

The chapel was dimly lit. It had a feeling of warmth and serenity, and the pressures he felt seemed to lessen by walking in.

For a moment he looked around. The inside was furnished differently from his own church. He walked slowly to the front and knelt before the altar as he had seen others do in pictures. How natural it seemed — not at all strange. The same peace he knew in his church came to him here.

With bowed head, he raised his plea for help to God. The inner peace known only to a Christian flooded his mind, stilling the doubts and fears. Plans that had seemed cloudy, cleared. The way forward opened. His course was laid out, and he knew what had to be done. It would not be easy, but the way was open.

God did want the youth center — a place for kids to bring their friends to laugh and play. It would have a bowling alley, swimming pool, tennis court. It would be a part of the church.

Getting up, he walked from the chapel with the perfect peace of a man who stands in the will of his God.

At the parsonage, Carolyn Lowell put the tea kettle on to heat. Little Diane was asleep, and Judd was due home soon. She always tried to have a snack ready when he got home from these late night visits, for it gave him time to relax before going to bed. And she had another, perhaps more selfish, reason. The moments they shared,

94

just the two of them, were few. She wanted to catch each one.

The back door banged opened. Judd bounced in and gave her a hearty kiss and hug.

"My, you're in a much happier mood than when you left. Your visit with Grant must have been enjoyable."

His enthusiasm lessened a bit. "Yes . . . it was a good visit, but not an enjoyable one. Grant gave me quite a lot to think about."

"Did he say something to encourage you?" she asked, wondering about his enthusiasm.

"No, the opposite." Judd pulled a chair out and sat down at the kitchen table. "In fact, he rather raked me over the coals. I guess with Grant we'll have to be more patient. We've planted the seed in his mind — the rest is up to the Lord."

Carolyn turned from the sink in such a hurry that she narrowly missed pouring boiling water on her hand. She stared at her husband. Could this be Judd? It didn't sound like him, for usually he was frustrated after talking with Grant. He wanted so much to lead him to Christ.

"That's not why I'm excited," Judd said as Carolyn turned back to the tea. "Grant helped me to decide that we're going ahead in building the youth center."

This time the tea kettle did bang to the counter, spilling water all around. Carolyn flew to the table and threw her arms around her husband. How long they had dreamed and planned together for this center.

"Oh, Judd, that's wonderful. When do we start?"

He laughed. "Not so fast, I only made the decision."

"How did you ever get the trustees to okay it?"

Again, his enthusiasm lessened a bit, showing her all was not what she first had expected. "I didn't exactly get the okay of the trustees, but I've got quite a plan to prove to them how much we need it."

Carolyn listened as he related the events of the evening. She felt the pain of Grant's accusation. She knew the doubts and fears that had attacked Judd. She understood his need for prayer and of finding the answer in the little chapel. The plan he had come up with was daring, but it could work.

When he finished his story, he waited for her comment. Carolyn reached out and touched his hand. "There's a chance, but nothing is gained without taking chances."

He had her approval. Abruptly, his mood changed. He had needed her for that moment, and now with her assurance, he was ready to go on. Carolyn pulled her hand back. She had been there when he needed her, but now she had to step out of his way.

Judd jumped to his feet. "I'm going to change clothes, then I'm going to the movies."

"Operation youth center begins," she called after him as he raced upstairs on his tiptoes.

Sunday morning, Judd stood up in the pulpit. Before he began his sermon, he looked out over the congregation. There was the usual settling down for the sermon. Men leaned back in the pews; mothers got pencils and papers out to keep little tykes busy; here and there an eyelid dropped heavily. A great love for these people leaped in his heart.

"Instead of the sermon I had prepared, I want to share with you an experience I had this week. It is connected with the case of three boys now awaiting trial."

Wavering attention snapped back to him. This was something of high interest. They had read the stories in the paper about their pastor. What was he going to say?

"Most of you, I'm sure, have read my interview by the press. The editor did take a few liberties with what I said, but one idea was reported correctly. I do not condemn those three boys for what they did . . . how can I? I'm responsible for the trouble they're in. . . ."

Judd paused long enough to let the impact of his words sink in. All eyes were locked upon him.

"I am guilty . . . and so are each of you. We are guilty of the murder of Harry Rosenthal. We are guilty because

96

of what we did, and perhaps moreso, for what we didn't do."

A feeling of uneasiness ran through the congregation. There was twisting and shuffling. Judd wondered if he had chosen his words wisely? Was he going too fast? It was too late to worry about that now.

"I attended a drive-in movie one night this week. The bill included 'Loss of Honor,' a movie for mature adults."

Here and there an eyebrow arched. Questioning glances met his. The theme of the movie was well-publicized and was not the movie for a minister to see.

"I didn't go there to see the film, which I consider trashy. I wanted to see who would attend such a movie and what their reaction would be."

Judd leaned out over the pulpit. "You would be shocked to know some of the people I saw there. Many of them are sitting right here this morning and not all of them are teenagers."

As he spoke, he looked back and forth across the pews. His eyes found many averted glances. It seemed as though more people had seen that movie than he realized. Was he too late? Was this already accepted?

"How many are innocent of reading the newest, hot best sellers? What about the off-color stories and the office incidents? Are any of us not guilty? And yet, do you realize what's happening to your minds, and what you're doing to your children?

"Oh, I know this stuff is labeled as being realistic and down to earth. Maybe it's time we take a good look at what it really is. It's nothing but trash put out by degenerate men who aren't capable of anything better. It does nothing but push us down in the gutter."

The people listened and some appeared ashamed. Was it enough? Had he said enough to make a difference, or would it be put on a shelf like so many other Sunday sermons?

"My friends, we can't stuff this trash into our minds and the minds of our children without being scarred, just as a man can't put on soiled clothes without getting dirty."

97

Judd stepped to the side of the pulpit. "I know I've been rough this morning. Preachers aren't supposed to preach like this any more, but this week I had a rude awakening to what we're allowing to go on in our city. Because of the things we take part in, and our laxity in not clearing some of it up, three boys are in jail for murder. Not only that, many more are headed there.

"Something has to be done and we're the ones who must do it. We have to go to work. We need to build a place where young people can come with their friends and have fun — a place where we can show the community that being a Christian is fun. We *have* to do these things. If Christian people won't accept the commands of Christ . . . if Christian people won't go to work for Him . . . if we've become so worldly that we can't work for Christ . . . then who in this world will?"

He had said it — the challenge was out. Now, what would their answer be?

The following Wednesday, after their weekly luncheon, Grant asked Judd if he'd like to go by and see Mrs. Templeton. "I haven't been to see her for a week. Want to come along?"

"Sure," Judd answered. "She's the one who saw the whole thing, isn't she?"

"Yes. I wish I could use her as a witness. For a reason I haven't been able to discover yet, she doesn't think the boys are guilty. But she's getting old and her mind wanders. She was upset by what she saw, and it's hard to sift the story from her."

"The whole thing must have been a shock to her."

"Yes, it took her a long time to recover," Grant said. "Her family is gone, so I've been watching after her."

"It's a shame you can't use her — the only witness, and she can't testify."

Mrs . Templeton was sitting by her front window when Grant drove up. She smiled and waved. "Come in, come in," she said, holding the door open as they came up the steps. "Oh, I'm so glad you came today. I have something terribly important to tell you."

"Well then, I'm glad I came, too," Grant said.

"And you've brought a friend. I know you," she said to Judd. "You're Reverend Lowell."

"Yes I am, Mrs. Templeton, and I'm happy to meet you."

"You two boys sit down and I'll fix some tea," she said turning toward the kitchen.

"No, don't go to all that trouble," Grant called after her.

She stopped halfway down the hall. "Nonsense. I don't often get guests. I want to enjoy you."

"Then at least let us come into the kitchen with you."

She had to consider this. Her mother had taught her that it was impolite to take guests into the kitchen. But, times had changed, she reasoned, and Mr. Williams was more than a guest, he was almost family. "All right, you may come in, but you must promise not to try and help."

Grant and Judd solemnly promised. She led the way to the kitchen. All the while she was fixing the tea, she kept up a steady stream of conversation. Sometimes she would talk of present times. Sometimes her thoughts would slip into the past. It was lively and humorous. Time passed swiftly. A cuckoo clock on the wall announced the hour and surprised them both.

"You know," Grant said, "we're going to have to go."

"Oh, must you?" Her voice pleaded with them to stay.

"We must," Grant said firmly, having experienced this prolonging before.

"Oh! Well, there was something I wanted to tell you. I thought it might be important."

"And what's that?"

Her brow creased in concentration as she tried to remember. She stood up and came to his side. "Oh, dear, I can't seem to remember what it was."

Grant stood up and hugged her. "That's all right. You'll think of it next time."

She nodded, but her disappointment remained. "Next time I must remember to write it down. Each time I'm so sure I won't forget."

"We'll come back soon," he promised.

The promise brought a smile to her lips. They helped her back to her place in the front room by the window. She waved as they left.

"What was she trying to remember?" Judd asked as they drove off.

"I don't know. It's come up before. She feels it's quite important, but she's never been able to tell me what it is."

"She could have the answer to the whole case and we might never find out what it is."

"Oh, one of these days she'll remember it," Grant said, not feeling as confident as he tried to sound.

CHAPTER EIGHT

The next morning Grant went into the office early. Louise was still there ahead of him. She handed him a telephone message, and watched his face for a reaction. The message was from the district attorney.

"When did Bob call?" he asked.

"Yesterday, while you were out."

"Did he say what he wanted?"

"Only that he wanted to talk to you as soon as possible," Louise replied.

It could mean only one thing. Bob had decided whether he would ask to have the case transferred to juvenile court from a criminal court. What was the answer going to be? It had been too long in coming and the evidence was stacked too strongly against the boys.

"All right, I'll call him now."

He took the note into his office and dialed the number. Bob answered.

"I've been waiting for your call, Grant."

"Sorry I'm so late. I didn't get back to the office last night."

"This doesn't come easy, and I want you to know that I've given it quite a bit of thought. But I'm going to have to ask at the hearing that the boys be tried as adults."

It was what Grant had expected, but he still fought it. "If it's granted, you know what it will mean?"

"Yes, Grant, but there is too much against them. If I

101

could have found anything in their favor . . . there's nothing I can do."

"Feelings are running high."

"I fully realize that — only too well," Bob said ruefully. "That's why I can't go along with you. The city wouldn't stand for it. I know it's hard on you, but my hands are tied."

"They'll never get a fair jury trial," Grant said.

"I will do everything I can to insure that, but I can't help you on the other." His voice was final.

"All right," Grant said simply. "Thanks for calling.

After hanging up, Grant sat only a moment, then called Louise on the intercom. It was settled — the hearing was soon. He had to keep the case in juvenile court. It was the only chance they had. "Bring in the file on the Rosenthal case," he asked. It was time to fight.

The problem seemed to center around the *Daily News*. The first step would be to soften their approach. Talking to Shadwell was a waste of time. If he were going to accomplish anything, he would have to go over Shadwell to the owner.

Grant found the owner's name and was preparing to call him, when the intercom rang.

"Judd's here," Louise announced.

"Send him in."

The door opened and Judd bounced in.

"You're looking pretty chipper," Grant said.

"I feel that way. I came over to tell you what happened at the church last night, but that can wait. Louise said you have a problem."

"The D. A. won't help me. He feels the public opinion is too strong against the boys. I was going to call the owner of the *Daily News* and see if he'll do something about Shadwell."

"I thought Shadwell was the top man."

"He runs the paper, but Conrad Welsey owns it."

The name brought a shocked look to Judd's face.

"Do you know him?"

Judd nodded. Yes, he knew Conrad Welsey. The man was a deacon in his church. How would he ever explain this to Grant? He knew exactly what his friend's reaction was going to be. How could a member of Grace Brethren let a man like Shadwell use his paper to hurt people so much. A sick feeling passed over Judd. Would Christians never realize that the world was watching them every minute?

"I know Conrad," Judd said at last. "He's a deacon at Grace Brethren."

"Oh."

"Come on, let's go see him," Judd said heading toward the door. "I'm sure he'll do something when we explain what's going on."

For an hour and a half, Grant and Judd drove around the city trying to catch Conrad Welsey. Every place they went they seemed to just miss him. Grant was ready to give up, but Judd was determined they would see the owner. Conrad had to come through.

Finally they went to Welsey's home, but even there they couldn't catch him. Judd left a letter at the house explaining what had happened and that he was seeking his help.

"Never mind," Grant said as they drove away. "I'll find some other way to get along."

"No, he'll come through," Judd said confidently, then prayed he wasn't making a mistake.

Conrad Welsey stood at the window and watched Lowell drive away with his lawyer friend. They hadn't been able to catch up with him because he didn't want them to. He knew what they wanted. He had been expecting them. At first he had panicked, because he didn't want to get involved. Now he had had time to think, and still he had turned away. He knew what had to be done, but he refused to do it. He was a coward.

Conrad left the house and walked out to the garage. The chauffeur started toward him, but Conrad waved him

103

away. He wanted to drive alone. Sometimes driving helped him clear his mind — it helped ease his problems.

This time driving didn't help. This wasn't just another problem. He had to decide what he believed — which side was he going to be on?

He pulled into a filling station far outside of town. No matter how far he went, he wasn't going to look any better in his own eyes. He didn't want to fight; he wanted things to run smoothly without a lot of work on his part. He wanted to be left alone, and yet he realized that this couldn't be.

His father always had called him a weakling, and he still couldn't stand on his own two feet. Because of this he had let down his good friend, a man who had helped him so many times. Once, just once, he wished he'd have the nerve to stand up for something instead of always running away.

If he hadn't listened to the crowd he wouldn't have gotten into this mess. His paper had been ailing for some time, when a friend had told him about Shadwell. A little checking had told him all about the editor, and no reputable paper would hire him. But Conrad had needed a strong man to run the paper and put it back on its feet, so he had hired the man. Once the paper was making its way, Conrad felt he could always let him go.

Shadwell took over the paper. At first his editorials and features hadn't been too bad. Conrad hadn't agreed with them, but sales improved. Then the Rosenthal murder hit the front page and everything broke loose — sales leaped.

With misgivings, Conrad watched the case progress. He was enough of a newspaperman to see what Shadwell was doing. It was the worst kind of sensationalism. This time the editor had gone too far, but still Conrad did nothing. Now Reverend Lowell was involved. Conrad couldn't stand back and watch; he had to do something.

It wasn't his fault, he argued against his conscience. He had tried to handle the business. He just didn't have the will and determination of his father and grandfather.

When his father had died, Conrad had tried to run all the family interests, but he couldn't manage it. He didn't want to sell the paper because it had always been in the family. It wasn't his fault Shadwell was such a stinker. If he had sold the paper he wouldn't have had any more say. Now, there was nothing else he could do.

As he was about to leave the filling station, he saw a phone booth. It was so close. All it would take was a telephone call to end the whole thing. If only he had the nerve. "Dear Lord, Please help me to do what's right this once."

The words seemed to come out of their own accord, but suddenly the way was clear. It was so simple. He wasn't fighting alone. That had been his problem all along. But he wasn't alone — he had Christ. Christ was with him and he could win. All he had to do was to let his Lord help.

With a growing feeling of excitement, he got out of the car and crossed over to the booth. As he fumbled for coins, a tightness grew in his chest. "Lord, help me," he prayed again, then entered the booth. He pushed the door shut and called the number of the paper. His hand was shaking, but he knew this time he would win.

At the newspaper, Shadwell was working in his glassed-in office when the intercom buzzed. His secretary announced an incoming call from Mr. Welsey. Shadwell frowned. What could the old man want now? He didn't want him to start meddling, just when things were going his way.

When he picked up the receiver, Shadwell carefully concealed all traces of annoyance in his voice. "Hello, Mr. Welsey. I'm glad you called. My secretary gave me the figures for last month's circulation. They're good."

Usually this worked to distract Conrad, but not today. "That's fine," he answered impatiently. "I called to talk about the reporting of the Rosenthal case."

Shadwell knew what was coming and tried to steer away. "That's about run its course," he said. "People are getting tired of it. I think I'll drop it."

"I want you to reverse your position on it," Conrad said.

"What! I can't do that."

"That's what I want you to do."

"Wait a minute. I'm not going to tell everyone I was wrong. Let's just let the story die."

"No, I want the story reversed."

"Now listen, Welsey, we had a certain agreement. . . ."

"You're fired."

The words exploded across the line, leaving a stunned party at both ends. Shadwell couldn't believe that Welsey could act so strongly. "But what . . ."

"You can leave immediately," Conrad continued. His words had shocked him, but he was sticking to them.

"Do you realize what you're doing?" Shadwell demanded.

No, Conrad thought to himself, but he wasn't going to let Shadwell know that. "I know exactly what I'm doing. I'm only sorry I didn't do it sooner."

"You can't run this paper without me. You'll go broke in two month's time."

"Then I'll have to go broke," Conrad said quietly.

Shadwell slammed down the receiver.

It was nearly evening by the time Conrad reached the *Daily News* building. One telephone call was about to change his whole life. Now it was time to go to work, for the paper needed an editor. Until he had time to find the right one, he was going to take control himself. This time when he hired an editor, he was going to precede the move with prayer. His Lord had pulled him from a jam once, he couldn't expect it again.

The first thing he wanted to do was call the whole staff together and tell them what was happening. He asked the department heads to call everyone for a meeting. For awhile Conrad was alone in the office filled with old memories. He sat down at the desk. It all seemed so familiar. How many times had he seen his father bent over

106

this desk. He had worked at this desk himself, but it had never seemed as comfortable as it did now. He was ready to accept the responsibility.

There was one last battle to win. The crew of any newspaper was a proud and independent bunch. He had to win them to his side. He had to convince them that he knew what he was doing and shared their pride in their work.

Conrad left his office and walked out into the main room. The writers and reporters had all left for the called meeting. He walked down the empty aisles between the muted typewriters, the scattered copy and the smudges of ink. A tightness grew in his chest as he suddenly realized how much he loved all this.

"Lord, please give me another chance to build this up," he whispered, then started to the meeting.

The buzz of conversation halted when Conrad entered the room. All eyes focused on him. He walked the length of the room to the platform at the end. He climbed up the steps and turned to face his employees confidently. He looked down into a sea of waiting faces. Some were friendly, some were curious, but none were hostile.

"For those of you I haven't met, my name is Conrad Welsey. I'm the owner of the Daily," he began. "I don't intend to bore you with a long speech, but there are two things I want to tell you."

A smile flickered across a few faces. He had started right.

"The first point I'm sure you already are aware of. Mr. Shadwell no longer works here. I can only say that I'm sorry he ever did."

He paused, not sure how to continue. Would they accept what he wanted to say next or would they resent him for saying it?

"The second point some of you know. I am going to take over the position of editor personally. I hope you don't misunderstand or feel that I'm trying to push my beliefs off on you, but I intend to reestablish the high Christian standards this paper once had. My grandfather and my father ran a successful paper with these principles, and I think I can, too."

There was moving about and a surprised look on many faces. It hurt Conrad to see how far he had fallen. These people were surprised to hear that he was a Christian.

"I am a Christian," he stated firmly, "and I'm going to run the paper with these convictions. If any of you feel you cannot work under these conditions, I will understand. You'll be given a severance pay and a good recommendation."

He paused again. The mood in the room seemed to have changed. The people now seemed closer. There was a feeling of acceptance, and, yes, he felt a small bit of respect.

"I won't keep you longer," he said. "Your decision is your own. I promise I'll work hard. Between us we should be able to come up with a newspaper we can all be proud of."

He stepped from the platform, and a round of applause greeted him. His face turned red, but there was pride in his step as he left the room.

Evening passed into morning. Except for a few minutes of sleep caught on a couch, Conrad hadn't left his work. There were so many decisions to make. With the first edition, he wanted the city to know there was a change in the *Daily News*.

He returned to his office and sank into the leather desk chair. A wave of exhaustion swept over him. The beginning had been made. The paper would be out on time and he could be proud of the work.

After a few minutes of relaxation, he picked up the telephone. Soon he would have to go home to sleep. His mind was too foggy to make clear decisions, but first he had to share his victory with the one man who could really appreciate it. He called Reverend Lowell.

Judd was in his study when the call came through. He recognized the caller, but was only mildly surprised. He

108

knew Conrad would come through. Without explaining, Conrad asked him to come down to the office of the *Daily News*. The man's voice was weary, but there was a note of victory that prompted Judd's quick agreement.

After hanging up, Judd stayed by the telephone. The call from Conrad could mean only one thing. He had made his decision and had won his battle. If this were true, Judd wanted another man to witness what had happened. He wanted to show Grant that, in the end, Christ always proved sufficient and did hold the answers.

Within the hour, Judd and Grant arrived at the *Daily News*. Walking to the editor's office, they felt the vibrating excitement that filled the building. Grant wondered about it, but Judd knew what was happening. They found Welsey in his office, bent over a proof. His coat and tie were in a heap over a chair; his hair was messed and he needed a shave; but a radiance seemed to explode from him.

He jumped to his feet when the two men entered. The lines around his eyes were etched in weariness, but his voice was filled with excitement.

"Pastor, Mr. Williams, come in! Please excuse my untidy appearance. I'm glad you could come!"

Grant was surprised by the enthusiasm of the greeting. He didn't know Welsey very well, but his opinion, based on the actions of the previous day, wasn't very complimentary. There seemed to have been a complete change. Not only this, but Grant could see no sign of Shadwell.

"Your plant seems busy this morning," Judd commented.

"It is," Conrad confirmed. "We had to work a full crew all night to get the first edition out on time. Now we've started redoing the Sunday edition."

Conrad saw a quick glance pass between Grant and Judd. He understood the meaning.

"I deliberately avoided you yesterday because I was afraid to face you. For a long time I've known that the position the *News* was taking was wrong, but I was too much of a coward to do anything about it. You made me see how much I was failing my Christ."

109

Grant listened in avid interest. It wasn't easy for any man to admit he was wrong. The stand Conrad was taking was even more amazing. There was nothing in his stand that Grant could argue with. This was what the man believed, and he was going to stand by his decision. Grant wondered — had he been selling Christianity short? It certainly had changed this man.

Judd watched Grant to see the effect the editor's words would have upon him. The lawyer was impressed. The personal statement of a Christian far surpassed all the preaching Judd could do. When a man was telling what had actually happened to him, there was just no way to argue with him.

"It's hard for me to admit I was wrong," Conrad concluded, "but I have been and I intend to do something about it. And I intend to see that this city hears the truth about your case, Mr. Williams."

Grant only hoped it would be in time.

Time was running out. The hearing was only days away, and Grant was growing more apprehensive. Never before had he been so sure of a client's innocence or so unsure of his ability to help him.

So many things were going badly. The change in attitude of the *Daily News* was having success, but time was so short. Would people change their thinking that fast? The evidence and motive Grant needed weren't to be found. He was even beginning to doubt the law. After a lifetime of work and devotion, was the law going to fail?

Friday evening as he was leaving, Louise invited him to a meeting at Grace Brethren Sunday afternoon. She sensed his discouragement. She felt if he saw what the church was doing to help the young people, he might feel better. He told her he would think about it, but he really didn't plan to go.

When Sunday came he was feeling no better. He thought about Louise, that she wanted him to go to the meeting. He didn't want to go. All he felt like doing was running away from the trial that was coming closer and closer.

He thought of Doris. He had been avoiding her lately until he had a chance to think a few things out. She had a way of making him do and want things he shouldn't have, but maybe today she was what he needed. A ride in the country and a quiet dinner sounded inviting. Maybe she was free.

She answered the phone. Her voice was refreshing, and immediately he was glad he called. "What are you doing today?"

"Not a thing. Sundays are bad for me. With Gary gone it gets lonely in the apartment."

"How about a ride and dinner?"

"Sounds great."

"Pick you up in fifteen minutes."

"Oh, dear, I'll never be ready. Never mind, come anyway and you can read the paper while you wait."

Right on schedule, Grant arrived at her apartment. There was a delay in her answering his ring. "I warned you," she said as she let him in, "I'm not ready. You'll have to sit down and read the paper while I finish."

"Well now, let me see." He stepped around her. "You look fine to me. However, if you want to spend more time appeasing your vanity, I'll wait."

"Oh, go sit down," she said, giving him a push toward the living room.

He went in and sat down on the couch. He picked up a section of the *Daily News*. Welsey had won his battle. The Daily seemed to be doing fine. Judd was also winning his battle. From what Louise had said, the church was back of him on the youth center and construction was going to start immediately. Why couldn't he win his battle? The law had always been enough before. Why did he doubt it now?

Absently he began paging through the paper. Doris came in, and watched him without speaking. His face appeared tight and drawn. He was turning the pages, but he wasn't reading. Something was troubling him. It had to be the case. The hearing was soon, and it must not be going well. Her son's trial for murder wasn't going well. The thought almost made her scream. She hadn't allowed herself to think about it or the possible outcome – she had to do everything in her power to free Gary.

Had she done everything? There was one thing remaining. She had thought of the plan some time ago, and it would work if Grant would accept it. There was a chance. In the beginning she wouldn't have hesitated, but now she had much more to lose. Her feelings for Grant were more involved than she had planned.

"Before you get too comfortable, we'd better go."

He jumped to his feet. "You're right. Already I'm so relaxed I could fall asleep. Let's go."

He helped her on with her jacket and they left the apartment. In the car, driving away from the city, Grant's spirits seemed to lighten with each passing mile. It always happened this way when he was driving with her. She helped him to forget.

For Doris it was the opposite. Her mood grew darker, for she had made a decision. Because of her son, she had to do it. It was too late for her to change, and this was the only way. If only he would understand.

After a while, Grant noticed her quietness. He tried to tease her but she didn't respond. Finally he reached out and took her hand. "What's the matter, Doris?"

"Nothing, I'm just tired. The strain has been building up." Why, oh, why, couldn't she use him as she had others and then forget him?

"I'm being inconsiderate," he said. "You put on such a brave front I sometimes forget what you're facing."

"I don't feel very brave right now," she said with a little laugh.

He squeezed her hand again. "Want to stop and talk for a while?"

"I . . . yes, I think I'd like that."

112

He pulled off the road into a rest area. "Now, tell me what's the matter. Is it Gary?"

She nodded. "The trial is soon."

"The hearing is this week, unless I can win a delay."

"It hasn't been going well has it?"

This question he didn't want to answer but he had no choice. Lying wasn't going to help her. "At the moment, Doris, the case is not going as I'd like it to. There are too many unanswered questions. We would profit much by a delay."

"Is a motive one of the questions?"

Grant looked at her sharply, and she refused to meet his eyes. "That's one of the questions."

"If things don't go right, what will happen to Gary?"

Why was she torturing herself? Grant wondered if she had been trying to fool herself all along. By now she should know what would happen.

"I want to know, Grant."

"All right, Doris. I won't keep anything from you. If things go right, Gary could be sent to a correction home until he is twenty-one. That is, if the case remains in juvenile court. If it goes to a criminal court, under the present charges he could get life."

Doris caught her breath. This was more than she had prepared herself for. Life in prison. She shook her head. "No, Grant, not jail. Gary can't go to jail. That really wouldn't happen; would it?"

Grant took her hands. "Get hold of yourself."

"He can't go to jail. You understand, don't you? Gary's my son. I raised him. He's not a bad boy. He doesn't deserve jail. It's my fault, not Gary's."

"Be quiet and listen to me!" Grant demanded. The sharpness in his voice stopped her. "It's going to be all right. Everything will work out," he said, wishing he could believe his words.

Tears fell from her eyes. "I've tried to believe that

113

everything would come out all right, but I can't pretend any more."

Grant held her hand in his. Her tears upset him. He had always thought of her as such a self-sufficient person. Now she seemed helpless and alone.

"Grant, isn't there anything we can do to save him?"

He sighed, showing more hopelessness than he really wanted her to see. "We've done all we can."

"Can't we do something to win the judge's sympathy? So he'll keep the case in juvenile court?"

"We've been doing that right along. With the change in the papers, we might have more of a chance. I wish we had more time, though."

She hesitated before speaking again. This was the time to spring her plan. Since the first meeting with Grant, she had been working toward this idea. What was his reaction going to be?

"If Gary had a good reason for wanting that money, would this make the judge more sympathetic toward him?"

A good reason. A motive. This was what he had been searching for right along. "A lack of motive has been the weakest point in our defense."

Her voice was very quiet as she continued. "Suppose they stole the money to give it to someone who needed it?"

This was the answer he needed, but for some reason he didn't feel elated. He felt only a growing suspicion. "Who needed the money?"

"I did. I need an operation. Gary found out about it. He was trying to get the money for me."

"What kind of an operation?"

"My doctor will explain."

It was wrong. Too many questions were popping into his mind. Why had she waited so long in telling him? With all her connections, why couldn't she have gotten the money? Why had Gary involved all the other boys? Why had all the boys lied about it? There were too many questions.

"Why didn't you come and tell me before?"

She was ready with an answer. "I didn't want anyone to know. I know it was foolish, but I didn't realize how serious the whole thing was."

This was exactly what Grant needed to build his case around — a sympathetic motive. With Doris to testify, he stood a good chance of winning. Only one thing stood in the way — she was lying. What was he going to do? Her offer was tempting. Considering all the harm done the boys by Shadwell, this could even the scales. He was ready to try anything to get the boys a fair deal. If this was what it took, then he should do it. It was only fair. They were good boys and deserved another chance. It wouldn't be like he was turning hardened criminals loose.

Still, he couldn't do it. When the law had to depend on lying and deceit for justice, then something was wrong. The system had failed. No, this wasn't what he needed.

"Doris, without a doubt what you have told me would be a tremendous help. There is one question that I must ask you before I use it. Is what you told me the truth?"

Doris sat up straight. She seemed to move away from him. The point had been reached. There could be no turning back. She felt a moment of panic. So much was at stake. Gary had to come first.

"I have a close doctor friend. He will testify that I need the operation."

Grant looked at her. She still refused to meet his eyes. Silently she waited, her face void of expression. The feeling of compassion faded, and he saw her for what she was: a cold, calculating woman who had used him. She wasn't for him. There had to be more to life than what she was offering.

"Doris, I won't remember what you have said to me. I'd like to believe that you're under a great strain and aren't thinking clearly. We'll pretend it didn't happen."

She slumped back against the seat. The gamble had lost. She had failed to save her son, and had lost the one she had come to love. Instead of bitterness, she felt only emptiness. A tiny door had opened, giving her a

115

glimpse of what life could be. She had closed the door.

"Would you take me home?"

He looked at her. Misery was written in her face. "Of course," he answered. He couldn't even feel sorry for her. He wanted only to get away from her and the offer he had been tempted to accept.

After leaving Doris, Grant passed Grace Brethren on his way home. A number of cars were parked around the church. He remembered the meeting Louise had asked him to attend. Perhaps what they believed to be true was foolishness to him, but at least it gave aim and purpose to their life. Or was it foolishness? So far Judd had been right. Life could be so much simpler if a man could believe.

The time wasn't right. Grant turned away. He wanted so desperately to help the boys. Wouldn't he be given the chance? It seemed everything he tried turned out wrong.

For the first time in many years, Grant woke with a feeling of panic. The hearing was tomorrow, and so many questions remained unanswered. The clear-cut motive had developed into a complexity of reasons. He wasn't even sure if he understood the boys and why they had acted as they had. What was going to happen? How was it going to end? He didn't know.

Today he wanted to go by the jail and talk with the boys. He wished he could have made them more interested in what could possibly happen to them.

At the jail, he stopped a few minutes with each boy. Beneath their cloak of unconcern, he seemed to feel a certain fear and question. Perhaps as they faced the judge they would understand what they had done. Perhaps then they could understand that their lives weren't really meaningless. But by then it would be too late.

Back at the office he opened the door and went in, an automatic smile on his lips. Louise wasn't there to accept his greeting. Her desk was empty. He glanced at his watch, and noticed she should have been there. Where was she? He felt a moment of concern. Had something happened to her? The door to his office was open. In the time it took him to cross the room, many wild thoughts flashed through his mind. Had someone broken into his office? Had something happened to her? He couldn't take that.

At the door he stopped. Louise was standing at the window gazing out across the city. Relief and tenderness swept over him. She wasn't gone — she was here. It was always like this. Whenever he was discouraged and needed help, she was there — always dependable — always waiting to help him. It would be nice having someone like that around all the time. The thought startled him. How easy and natural it had come to his mind. Could it be?

He crossed the room. She didn't hear him until he was next to her. Then she turned and smiled up at him. "You caught me daydreaming," she confessed with a blush. She didn't add that she had been dreaming about him.

"It's good to dream a little," he answered.

She turned back to the window and watched the street below. "So many things have happened. I wonder if it will ever be the same when this case is over?"

"I don't think it will."

She felt his discouragement. Lightly she touched him on the arm. "Grant, don't be discouraged. You believe that right and justice will overcome wrong and crime. With a couple of prayers from my side thrown in for good measure, things will work out."

He forced a smile to his lips. "I wish I could feel your confidence."

You can, she wanted to say. All you have to do is believe. But the time wasn't right to say it.

"Were there any messages?" he asked, turning to his desk.

"Reverend Lowell called a while ago. He would like you to call him."

"All right. Get him on the line," Grant asked.

A short time later, the young minister's voice came booming across the line. "Grant, I'm glad you called. I wanted to talk to you."

117

"About what?"

"The hearing tomorrow — I want to be there."

This was what Grant had thought, but he didn't want Judd there. He didn't want to expose the minister to any more abuses. "I don't think it's a good idea, Judd. It won't do you any good to be seen with me."

Judd had a ready answer. "Let me be the judge of that. I think by now everyone knows where I stand. And from the way my people have been working, they're behind me."

Grant sighed. He was not going to be able to convince his young friend differently. "All right, Judd, I'll pick you up on my way to court."

The day passed slowly. Grant wandered in and out of the office. He flipped through the pages of his brief, wondering if he could possibly have overlooked something, but knowing all the while that he hadn't.

Several times Louise looked up to find him watching her, a questioning look on his face. Each time she caught him, he would smile sheepishly then hurry away. Finally in the afternoon Louise went into his office.

"Grant, why don't you go home?"

He looked up at her in surprise, wondering how she could suggest such a thing. "I have work to do."

"So do I, and with you wandering around, I can't get a thing done."

He laughed. "Am I really that bad?"

"Yes, I'm afraid you are."

"Oh, all right. I really don't have anything to do. I'll get a few things together."

He went back to his desk to pack the things needed for the hearing the next morning. Louise followed him a few minutes later and found him standing by the window, his hands clasped behind his back. "I wish I could get a delay. Though even if I could, I'm not sure that it would do any good."

"It's going to come out okay," she said.

118

Grant shook his head. "Not this time. These boys aren't going to get the chance they deserve."

"Well, there is one last course open," Louise said.

"What's that."

"You could direct a few prayers heavenward on your own." Her voice was light, but there was a deep meaning in her words.

A smile of resignation filled his face. "Louise, I'd even be willing to get down on my knees if I thought that it would help those boys."

Louise started to reply, then stopped. It wasn't time to say more. She would wait and let the words sink in. One day he would see how much he needed Christ. Then she would tell him of the One to whom she had given her life.

"I guess I'll take your advice and go home." He looked at her a long time, wishing he had her inner strength and assurance. Then he turned away.

After a nearly sleepless night, Grant arrived at the office. At last it was going to end. He felt relief, and at the same time a little sick. There was nothing more he could do to get ready. He had tried very hard but the trust and faith hadn't paid off. So many things had happened. His trust in the law had been shaken. It wasn't the great power he had believed.

Soon it was time to leave for the court. Louise was already there getting things in order. He glanced around to be sure nothing had been forgotten. Of course he found nothing. Louise was very thorough. Louise . . . saying her name left him with a warm comfortable feeling. After all these years, was he going to fall in love with her? First it was Doris, and now Louise. Was he getting old? Why did he feel so alone? There wasn't time to worry about that.

He left his office and started for the hall door. As he passed Louise's desk, he noticed the top drawer was open. Louise was so neat, this surprised him. He reached across the desk to close the drawer. As he did, he noticed a book on top of a stack of papers. It was a Bible, and he smiled. How well she knew him. This was a reminder. He picked it up and held it tight.

"Little book, she puts a lot of faith in you and what you say. I wish I could. Those boys could use some help. I don't understand all she says, but if you could see fit to lend a hand, we'd appreciate it. Then maybe I could understand."

He paused. Louise had said a little prayer might help. It worked for them. Could it work for him? It certainly couldn't hurt.

"Lord, help me to get these boys the fair chance they deserve, and help them to straighten out their lives."

Quickly he glanced around, wondering if anyone had overheard him. No one was around. He put the Bible back in the drawer, and it left a strange warm glow in his hand. He wondered. . . .

As he straightened up, the telephone rang. It came so unexpectedly that he jumped. For a moment he debated answering. If it was a client, he didn't want to get involved. It could be Judd making sure he wasn't forgotten. It could even be Louise calling about some forgotten paper. He picked it up.

The call was from Mrs. Templeton. She sounded excited and out of breath. "Oh, I caught you. I must see you now."

Annoyance flickered through his mind. He felt sorry for her, but he didn't have time today. "It's good to hear from you, but I can't talk. I'm on my way to court. . . ."

"I know, but I must see you," she insisted.

"Mrs. Templeton, the hearing is today. I have to be in court in a little while."

"Oh, dear. I do hope things work out for the boys. It will only take a minute for you to stop."

Grant felt like throwing his hands up in dismay. He dearly loved the old lady, but at times she could be exasperating. When she wanted to see him, she was incapable of accepting no for an answer.

"How about tonight?" he suggested. "If I came after supper, we'd have more time to talk."

"It's really important."

Grant saw he was wasting more time arguing than if he hurried on his way and stopped for a minute. "All right, I'll come for a minute. But remember, I can't stay."

Now if Judd would only be on time, Grant thought to himself, he could still make it.

Mrs. Templeton tried to hurry to answer the front door. It hurt her to walk fast, but she remembered that Mr. Williams had said he would be in a hurry.

"Come in," she greeted, swinging open the door. "I put the tea in the parlor. Hurry, so it won't get cold."

"I told you we can only stay a minute," Grant reminded.

"I remember, but you can drink one cup while I talk."

Grant shrugged, and followed her into the parlor. Mrs. Templeton sat between Judd and Grant and poured the tea. "Lemon or sugar?"

"Sugar," Grant said.

"Sugar and a bit of lemon," Judd answered.

"How nice," she said, handing a cup to Judd. "That's the way my husband used to drink it."

The reference to the past caused Grant to wince. Sometimes when she thought of past happenings, her mind slipped into the past and she couldn't remember what she had meant to tell him.

Grant's fears were groundless. Today she was alert and determined to explain why she called. "There's one thing that really seems to bother me," she began. "The newspapers keep making the same mistake over and over in their story. Maybe it's a small mistake and doesn't matter, but I've always felt the papers have a responsibility to print the news as accurately as possible."

Grant assured her that he felt the same way.

"Maybe you can straighten them out. They insist on saying that the boys brought that terrible gun with them to the store. That isn't true."

Grant bit his tongue to keep from shouting. Even Judd recognized the possible significance of what she had said. They had to be careful not to overexcite her because she sometimes lost her trend of thought when she got excited.

"I wondered where the gun came from," Grant said casually."

"All you had to do was ask anyone around here," she answered. "All the older folks would know. It belonged to poor Marvin Clark. He brought it back from the war. Whenever he ran out of money, he would give it to Mr. Rosenthal to hold until his check came."

Grant hardly dared to hope it could be true. This one thing could completely change the case. They had searched for the owner of the gun so long. How could they possibly have missed finding this out? He asked her again if other people knew about this.

"Oh, yes," she assured him. "Mrs. Greenly and I were talking yesterday. We both agreed that this terrible thing would never have happened if it had been any other time of the month. The next day Marvin would have claimed the gun."

Grant jumped up and kissed the old lady soundly on the cheek. Promising to explain later, he grabbed Judd and pulled him out the door. They were in the car and pulling away from the curb before Judd had a chance to speak.

"What's all the panic?" he finally got out.

"Have to get hold of the district attorney. If he knows this, he might agree to a delay to trace down the evidence. Right now a delay could save those boys. It would give things a chance to quiet down. With the paper on our side, public opinion could change. We might have a chance."

"Maybe this is what she has been trying to tell you all this time."

"Maybe," Grant said. *And if I had left a minute*

sooner. If I hadn't seen the open drawer, what would have happened, he wondered.

At the courthouse, Grant and Judd scurried off in opposite directions in search of Louise and the district attorney. Grant found Louise at the door of the courtroom.

"We've got it," he cried, rushing up to her. He grabbed her and hugged her.

"Got what?" Louise blinked in surprise.

The words tumbled out in a maze. Stopped at the desk. Telephone rang. Rushed to Templeton's. She remembered. Know whose gun. Win delay. Judd find D. A. Paper change people. Judge listen.

Somehow, through the confused torrent, Louise suspected that because of a phone call, Grant had found some evidence concerning the gun that would win the delay and give the newspapers a chance to soften public opinion.

Before she had a chance to ask any questions, Grant grabbed her hand and pulled her down the hall in search of Judd and the district attorney.

They found the two men standing on the porch in front of the courthouse. Bob Matson was listening intently to what Judd was saying. He looked at Grant as the lawyer came up. Judd finished his story. They waited for Bob's answer.

Bob started to say something then stopped. He couldn't find the words. He had been wrong. He had let the newspaper and public opinion sway him from a path he knew he should follow. This was something he had sworn he'd never do.

"Grant . . . I'm sorry," he said at last. "Your boys do deserve more of a chance than I've given them. Thank God you stopped me." He paused again. There was nothing more he could say. "I'll go see about a delay." He turned and walked away.

The three looked after him. He was a good and honest man. He had made a mistake, now, at last, they had made him see and they had a chance.

"I'm going to call Conrad," Judd said. "With this

123

news, he can start showing people the other side of the story."

Grant and Louise were left alone on the courthouse porch. They stared out over the city. So much had happened, much more than this city would ever know. A serious trend had been stopped. Maybe now the trend of unconcern would swing the other way. The way Judd's people were responding, it might happen. If the city could just get interested in not only giving his kids a place to play, but also giving them something to do, then what happened would not all be tragedy.

"What will happen to the boys now?" Louise asked.

Grant thought. "Well . . . if we keep the case in juvenile court, they'll go before a judge and will probably be sent to a correction home until they're twenty-one."

Louise shook her head. "What a terrible shame — and so senseless. Whose fault was it, Grant?"

He shrugged. "All of ours. This time guilt has many faces — yours, mine, the boys, the whole city. The boys will suffer, but maybe we'll wake up."

"I guess it's a good thing the phone call came when it did. Otherwise, it would have been much worse."

Grant started to think. Pausing at the desk drawer . . . saying the prayer . . . the telephone ringing right then.

His eyes met hers. "Louise, many things have been happening. The change in Conrad — finding out about Doris — the telephone call." He wondered . . . could that prayer . . . perhaps Judd was right after all.

He reached out and again took her hand. "Louise, I want to ask you some questions about . . . about this Christ of yours. Maybe I do need Him."

He squeezed her hand tightly. She smiled through the tears of joy in her eyes. After all these years of waiting and praying — it was finally happening.